Astrid
the
Unstoppable

Astrid
the
Unstoppable

Maria Parr

translated from Norwegian by Guy Puzey
illustrated by Katie Harnett

CANDLEWICK PRESS

Copyright © 2009 Det Norske Samlaget, Oslo
Originally published as *Tonje Glimmerdal* by Maria Parr
with Det Norske Samlaget, Oslo
Published by agreement with Hagen Agency, Oslo
English-language translation copyright © 2017 by Guy Puzey
Illustrations copyright © 2017 by Katie Harnett

First US paperback edition 2020

Library of Congress Catalog Card Number 2018960078
ISBN 978-1-5362-0017-1 (hardcover)
ISBN 978-1-5362-1322-5 (paperback)

20 21 22 23 24 25 TRC 10 9 8 7 6 5 4 3 2 1

Printed in Eagan, MN, USA

This book was typeset in Berkeley Oldstyle.

Candlewick Press
99 Dover Street
Somerville, Massachusetts 02144

www.candlewick.com

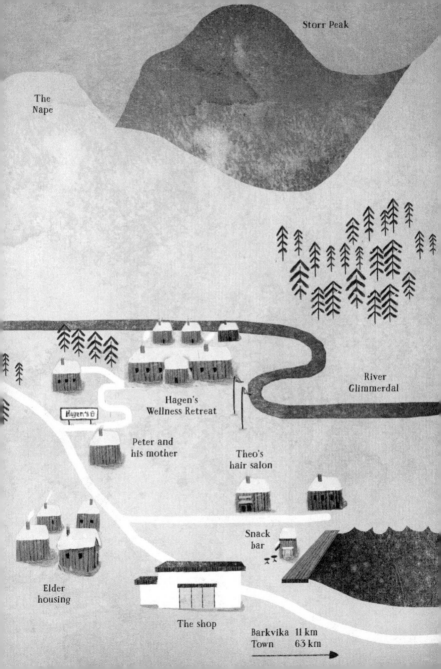

THE LETTER

As soon as you get off the ferry at the wharf, you'll feel the breeze blowing down from the glen. Even now, when it's winter and cold, you can still feel it. Close your eyes. You can smell the pine trees, and the spruce. Then just start walking.

Follow the road straight ahead, past the closed-down snack bar, the shop, and Theo's hair salon, and then keep going along by the river. The road starts off quite flat, with the odd house along the way. There's a digger parked outside one of the last houses. That's where Peter and his mom live.

Then there's more and more snow and trees, and fewer and fewer houses. The road narrows to half the width and becomes twice as steep. If you haven't been here before, you might hesitate, wondering if you've gone the wrong way. But you haven't. Because just as you start to wonder, you see a sign. GLIMMERDAL, it says. Then you know you're heading in the right direction after all.

The first thing you come to after the sign is a vacation camp. Listen carefully: whatever you do, don't enter that camp. If you do, don't come out saying you weren't warned. Klaus Hagen, the owner of Hagen's Wellness Retreat, is so sour he should be poured down the kitchen sink. He has no sense of humor, and he doesn't like children, especially if they make loud noises . . . and especially if they once smashed one of his cabin windows with a slingshot, even if it wasn't on purpose. He thinks those children are the worst. (The child who smashed that window isn't particularly fond of Mr. Hagen either, if truth be told. Sometimes she lies awake at night wondering whether she should smash another one.) So, if you've any sense at all, you'll head straight past Hagen's Wellness Retreat.

After Hagen's Wellness Retreat, you'll find yourself in some woods, where the snow bends the branches almost all the way down to your head. Some call it an enchanted forest. Just beyond it is Sally's green house, but there's nothing much enchanted *about that. You'll spot Sally's purplish perm sticking up from behind a potted plant in her living-room window. Sally will spot you too; you can be sure of that. Sally spots everything. Even if you were to sneak past that green house like a little mouse in winter camouflage, making not so much as a peep, Sally would still spot you. She never takes afternoon naps either.*

Once you're past Sally's house, you'll finally reach the bridge, the one that crosses the River Glimmerdal. If you turn right, go over the bridge, and walk a short way up the hill, you'll get to Gunnvald's farm. But if, instead of going right, you walk a short way up the hill to the left, you'll reach Astrid and her family's farm. There are no other farms up the glen, beneath the mountains.

So now you've arrived. Welcome to Glimmerdal.

5

CHAPTER ONE

In which Astrid almost skis a somersault

Cold February afternoons are very peaceful at the top of Glimmerdal. The river is quiet, because it's all iced up on top. There are no birds tweeting, because they've flown south. You can't even hear the sheep, as they're inside, in the barns. There's just the white snow, the dark spruce trees, and the tall, silent mountains.

But in the midst of this winter quiet, there was a black dot about to make some noise. The black dot was up at the foot of Cairn Peak, at the end of a long and quite uneven ski track. The dot was none other than Astrid Glimmerdal, with her lion's mane of curly red hair. Her father is a farmer here in Glimmerdal, and her mother is a marine research scientist who goes on expeditions, working along the coast and at sea. Her family has been living in the glen for a long time, which is why they share their surname with the place, as do some other families in the area.

Astrid was about to turn ten at Easter, and she was planning to have such a big party that it would be heard echoing all the way up the mountains.

Klaus Hagen, the one down at the vacation camp who doesn't like children, should really have been pleased with his lot in life. After all, there was only one child in the whole glen, and even Mr. Hagen should have been able to put up with just one. But he couldn't. Astrid Glimmerdal was precisely the type of child that Mr. Hagen couldn't stand. As soon as they met her, all his vacationing guests realized that even if they were staying at Hagen's Wellness Retreat, it was really Astrid's glen they were visiting. Luckily, the little empress of Glimmerdal was particularly fond of visitors.

"You should have 'welcome' printed on your forehead, Astrid," Auntie Idun had once told her.

In the winter, Astrid's ski tracks and footprints traced

lines and squiggles all across Glimmerdal.

"I let her out every morning and hope she'll come back in the evening," her dad, Sigurd, would say when visitors asked him where his daughter was off to now, as people in Glimmerdal always asked.

The little thunderbolt of Glimmerdal, that was what everyone called her.

Below Cairn Peak, Astrid shifted her weight a little, pointing the ends of her skis down toward the crag known as the Little Hammer. School had finished early, as it was the last Friday before winter break, so it was still the middle of the day.

"Ah, what a wonderful thing February vacation is," Astrid said to herself. "February vacation and downhill slopes."

The run down to the Little Hammer was steep. So steep that Astrid really had to steel herself. But this was what Auntie Eira and Auntie Idun did when they were home for Easter. They'd start from the same place and set off at a furious speed, kicking up a flurry of snow behind them like a bride's veil. They'd leap off the edge of the Little Hammer, flying sky-high. Auntie Eira even did somersaults.

"You need two things in life," Auntie Eira would say. "Speed and self-confidence."

Astrid thought those were wise words. While her aunts were away studying in Oslo, Astrid tried to keep in practice, doing lots of things that required speed and self-confidence.

One thing was certain, though—Astrid Glimmerdal would never even do so much as a tiny, sneaky little ski jump unless Gunnvald was sitting at his kitchen window, watching her. For a start, it's no fun jumping unless somebody's watching; and besides, it's a good idea to have somebody who can call the mountain rescue service if you don't get up again after landing.

Gunnvald lived quite a long way from the foot of Cairn Peak, but he had some fantastic binoculars. Now Astrid waved her arms to signal that she was ready.

And then the silence in Glimmerdal was broken.

"Old MacDonald had a farm!" Astrid sang, bellowing out the words and launching herself forward.

It is important to sing when you're skiing. Every time she jumped off the Little Hammer, Astrid sang so loudly that she started mini-avalanches in the hollow near the top of the Glimmerhorn.

"E-I-E-I-OOOO!"

She curled up with her hands in front of her and her head down to reduce the drag.

"And on that farm he had a cooooow!"

The edge of the Little Hammer was growing larger. Astrid began to sing extra loudly to stop herself from suddenly changing her mind, which might not end well.

"E-I-E-I-OOOO!" she sang so loudly that the words echoed off the mountains of Glimmerdal.

Holy muskrat, she was going fast! The Little Hammer was looming closer and closer. Good grief, why did she never learn? Why did she never, ever, *ever* learn? She was almost there. Soon she'd be going up. . . .

Astrid closed her eyes. There was the edge. She had butterflies in her stomach and her legs were tingling.

"With a moo-moo here and a moo-moooooooooooo . . . !"

Astrid was flying. She had never sung so much of "Old MacDonald" in midair. Blinking badgers, it was almost the whole chorus. If she'd known how to do somersaults, like

Auntie Eira, then she would've had time to do three in a row.

But I don't know how to do somersaults yet, Astrid thought while in midair. *Or maybe I do,* she thought next, when she noticed that her head was where her legs were supposed to be and her legs were where her head was supposed to be.

Then, after flying quite an impressive trajectory, Astrid crash-landed like an upside-down gummy bear in a cream cake with far too much cream. It was white and cold, and she didn't know whether she was alive or dead as she lay there. Gunnvald was probably wondering the same thing down at his kitchen window. Astrid lay still until she could feel her heart beating. Then she shook her head a little, as if to put everything inside it back in place.

"Does that count as a somersault?" she wondered aloud.

CHAPTER TWO

In which Gunnvald and Astrid talk about the olden days

Gunnvald lives in an enormous house and has a barn and sheep, like Astrid and her family. But there's always some kind of commotion with Gunnvald's sheep. They run off, and they die, and they eat Sally's tulips. Gunnvald also has a workshop. There he makes the most of his old age, earning some extra money to top up his pension by doing a bit of joinery. He's seventy-four years old and Astrid's best friend.

"Imagine being best friends with a stubborn old mule like him," Astrid says when she's feeling low. "Blinking badgers, there's not much of a choice here in Glimmerdal."

But deep inside, Astrid knows that Gunnvald would be

her best friend even if there were ten-year-old children living on every little patch of grass in the glen. She is so fond of Gunnvald that her heart creaks and groans at the thought of him. He's actually her godfather too. Astrid thinks it was brave of her mom and dad to let an old grumbler like him carry her at her christening. He might have dropped her slap-bang in the middle of the church if he felt like it. You see, Gunnvald can be so stubborn sometimes that you wouldn't believe it. Still, Astrid's mom and dad wanted it to be Gunnvald and nobody else. They put Astrid in his gigantic hands, and he hasn't let go of her since.

"What would you do without me, Gunnvald?" Astrid often asks him.

"I'd dig myself a big hole and jump in," Gunnvald answers.

When Astrid came gliding across the farmyard on her skis, Gunnvald moved the kitchen curtains aside with his binoculars and stuck his tousled head out into the winter air. He's as tall as a troll, with a slight stoop. In his prime, he was even taller—he's shrunk a bit over the past few years, what with his age and his arthritis and everything, but he never goes to the doctor. He's petrified of doctors. Besides, all Gunnvald needs is his fiddle under his chin, then he's as perky as a newborn calf. Gunnvald says there's no better medicine than that fiddle of his. What do you need doctors for when you've got a fiddle? A fiddle and a pinch of snus under your lip. Where Astrid and Gunnvald live, some grown-ups suck a kind of yucky tobacco powder called snus.

"Was that a somersault?" Astrid asked as she reached him.

Gunnvald huffed so hard that the curtains tugged at their rod. "If that was a somersault, Astrid Glimmerdal, then I'm an elk."

He asked if Astrid always had to land headfirst so that he thought she was dead. Astrid said that was exactly what she had to do.

In Gunnvald's kitchen, Astrid has a chair where she always sits, a peg where she always hangs her woolly hat, and a mug in the cupboard she always drinks from.

Hulda, Gunnvald's black-and-white cat, slunk past Astrid's legs as she made herself at home.

"It's finally winter break! Do you remember the olden days, Gunnvald?"

"Which olden days?" Gunnvald asked, putting a plate down in front of her.

Gunnvald had lived so long that, to him, the olden days could mean anything.

"The olden days before Klaus Hagen moved to Glimmerdal, when it was just a normal campsite down the road," said Astrid.

Yes, Gunnvald remembered those days well. "There was a heavenly hullabaloo every time people came on vacation," he reminisced.

"Children came in bucketloads," Astrid remembered. "All you had to do was go down to the campsite, and children were as easy to find as bilberries."

Gunnvald remembered that too. But then along had come the bad-tempered Klaus Hagen.

He came and saw Glimmerdal and thought it was a fantastic place. In fact, Mr. Hagen thought Glimmerdal was such a fantastic place that he went and bought the whole campsite. He's stinking rich. He built new cabins down there, and it looked so fancy that Astrid and everybody else in Glimmerdal thought it was brilliant. When he had

16

finished, he reopened it as a vacation camp. "Hagen's Wellness Retreat: the quietest in Norway," it said in his brochures. It was for people who wanted peace and quiet. To begin with, Astrid thought that was genius. Lots of people booked who needed a rest, and there was nothing nicer than visitors coming up to see where they lived in the mountains. But then Astrid began to wonder why on earth no children ever visited.

Astrid doesn't normally spend too much time wondering about things, so one day she cycled down to Mr. Hagen and asked him.

"Hey, Klaus, how come there's never any children at your camp?"

"Children aren't allowed at Hagen's Wellness Retreat," Mr. Hagen answered.

"Huh?" said Astrid.

"My guests want to hear the rushing river and the fresh breeze blowing through the spruce trees, not some horrible racket," Mr. Hagen explained, glancing at his watch.

Astrid looked at the vacation camp owner, dumb-founded. She decided that what he'd just said was the worst thing she'd ever heard in her whole life. But no sooner had she decided that than Mr. Hagen broke his own record by saying something even worse.

"Actually, what I said about horrible rackets applies to you, Asny."

"It's Astrid," Astrid corrected him.

"Astrid, right. Can you please stop singing at all hours of the day and night?"

Astrid scratched her ear. She couldn't believe what she was hearing.

"You destroy my guests' peace and quiet when you come screeching past on your bike," Mr. Hagen told her, putting on something that was possibly supposed to resemble a polite smile.

"Do you mean you want me to stop singing in my own glen?" she asked. Just to make sure.

"It's not exactly *yours*," Mr. Hagen muttered, annoyed. "In my advertisements I say that my camp's the quietest in Norway, and I would ask you to respect that."

That was probably the moment Mr. Hagen really took a wrong turn. You don't just go asking the little thunderbolt of Glimmerdal to stop singing. Anybody could have told him that. If only he'd asked them.

"No, sorry," Astrid replied. Then she plodded back up the glen, her opera singing practically flattening the trees by the side of the track.

Astrid kept on singing after that. In fact, she might even have started singing a bit more, if truth be told. Especially when she was biking past the camp. Mr. Hagen looked at Astrid almost as if she were some kind of small vermin. Things got even worse in the autumn, when Astrid was unlucky and broke a window at the vacation camp with her slingshot. She didn't mean to; she was aiming at the flagpole. It makes such a good sound when you fire your slingshot at flagpoles, and it's incredibly difficult to do. Even Astrid doesn't always score a direct hit when she aims at flagpoles.

"Oops," she said, as she heard the tinkling of broken glass.

She rode home at top speed and fetched all the pocket money she'd been saving. The money was in a beautiful small wooden box she'd made at Gunnvald's. She took the box to Mr. Hagen and solemnly said a big sorry.

But Mr. Hagen didn't want the box. He took out the money and gave her back the box with a grunt. "What would I want that for?" he asked, irritated.

What kind of a question was that? A rich man like him could keep it and put money in it, of course, Astrid thought. But Mr. Hagen snorted and closed the door.

That was the day Astrid gave up trying to be friends with Mr. Hagen. In fact, she gave up on Mr. Hagen altogether, from his topmost wisp of hair to his smallest toenail. How could anybody on earth say no to a box like that? She'd spent a whole Saturday with the wood-burning pen drawing two birds on the lid.

"That man knows nothing about art," Gunnvald said when she told him what had happened.

"He knows nothing about anything!" Astrid said angrily.

"That campsite is a sorry sight," Astrid said, back in the kitchen. "Not a single child on vacation. It's a good thing you've got me to liven things up, Gunnvald, otherwise you'd be stuck sitting here eating your dinner all alone."

Gunnvald bent his long body as he sat down on a kitchen chair, his knees and the wooden chair creaking together. "You're right there," he muttered.

They tucked into some fried potato dumplings, meat, and turnips. Astrid wondered what it was that always made Gunnvald's cooking tastier than any other food she had tried.

"Do you know what's ready for testing in there?" Gunnvald suddenly asked while he chewed, nodding in the direction of the workshop.

Silently Astrid put down her fork. "The sleds?"

CHAPTER THREE

In which Sled Test Run No. 1 is launched, and Astrid is threatened with a call to the police

Astrid and Gunnvald always have new projects in progress. But the one they were working on that winter really was the bee's knees. At least that's what Astrid and Gunnvald thought. They were designing the perfect steerable sled. They were going to make one that was as stable as a ferry, as fast as a motorcycle, and as beautiful as Gunnvald's late grandmother. If they could pull it off, they were planning to start full production of steerable sleds before next Christmas, which would make them as stinking rich as Mr. Hagen.

They'd had the idea one day when Astrid had been out with her toboggan.

"Rusty reindeer, toboggans don't have much oomph these days," she'd complained to Gunnvald.

"*Pfft*, toboggans!" Gunnvald had said. "What you need is a sled with runners that you can steer."

"Where can you get hold of one of those, then?" Astrid had asked.

"You can't get hold of proper steerable sleds anymore."

They'd have to get hold of one somehow, Astrid insisted, if it really was true that they were the best.

She was as sharp as a starling, Gunnvald thought, and she was right.

The next day he drove into town and came back with his pickup full of sled runners. Since then, Gunnvald had been welding, bending, and hammering away with gusto. They had a lot of things to test out if they were going to find what worked best. The sled they were going to make wouldn't be some shoddy piece of work; they were going to call it the Glimborghini. Astrid went from house to house, collecting all the wrecked sleds in the glen. Gunnvald said it was important to learn from previous manufacturers' mistakes.

"How's the sled making going?" people often asked.

"Oh, not too badly," Astrid and Gunnvald replied, trying not to let the cat out of the bag.

But now it had been several days since Astrid had last been in the workshop. She'd been busy with other things. She almost fainted with joy when Gunnvald opened the door, and there were three nearly finished sleds sitting on the floor in front of the sanding machine.

"What we need now is a test pilot. Preferably a child," Gunnvald murmured, looking across at Astrid, the only child in all of Glimmerdal.

Three steerable sleds at the top of a slope several kilometers long: it was such a glorious sight that it deserved to have an opera written about it. Gunnvald paced excitedly while Astrid tightened her bike helmet.

"By the time winter's over, we'll have a sled that can slide all the way down to the shoreline. I bet my snus tin on it," Gunnvald announced, his voice booming.

Astrid stood gaping. She hated snus, but besides that, it was four kilometers down to the shoreline, with flat parts, uphill stretches, and everything. Was it possible to go so far on a sled? Yes, Gunnvald thought it was, but not yet. First they had to do some testing and make a few calculations.

There were two types of brakes: a foot brake on one of the sleds and a lever on one of the others, which Astrid was to pull with her hand.

"What about the third sled?" Astrid asked, looking at the one that had just a steering wheel and no brakes.

"When we've found out which braking system works best, we'll install it on that one. Its runners are real corkers," Gunnvald said excitedly, rubbing his hands together.

He led her over and up onto the first sled. "This one might not turn as much as it should, but it's the brakes I'm most interested in to start with," he explained.

Astrid grabbed the steering wheel, and Gunnvald held up his walkie-talkie. They had to contact Peter before she set off so that he could stop the traffic.

Peter lives in the house with the digger outside. He's a friend of theirs, and he's in love with Auntie Idun. Auntie Eira told Astrid. But Peter's so shy that he never does anything about it—he just goes along the same, year in, year out. Watching it's enough to drive you crazy, according to Gunnvald.

"Test pilot ready. Over," Gunnvald grumbled into his walkie-talkie.

After some crackling and scratching, Astrid heard Peter's voice. "Traffic stopped. Over."

"Roger!" Gunnvald shouted, and before Astrid could gather her thoughts, the old man gave her a push with considerable force down the hillside.

Compared to tobogganing, this was something else. Astrid was down by the bridge before she could even think of the word *bridge*. She searched frantically with her foot for the brake. There was the pedal! She put her foot on it as hard as she could—too hard. The sled flew into a massive skid as it zipped across the bridge, sliding on only one runner. When she tried to come out of the skid, the sled tipped onto the other runner. It was impossible to stay in control.

"Woo-hoo!" Astrid shouted, and then, just as she was really getting going, she and the sled flew through the air like two strange birds and landed with a great *whomp* in the powdery snow.

For the second time that day, Astrid Glimmerdal found herself lying in deep snow, wondering whether or not she was still alive. Then she felt something scratching her face.

I'm still alive, she thought, struggling to lift her head out of the snow.

Blocking the daylight was a pair of narrow legs, and Astrid suddenly realized what it was that felt prickly against her face. Sally's poor rosebush. There it had been, lying under the snow all unsuspecting, when along flew Astrid Glimmerdal, waking it up from its winter slumber. Astrid lifted her gaze from Sally's legs to Sally herself. She was standing with her box of pills in one hand, looking suspiciously at the sled, now separated from its pilot.

"What in heaven's name are you up to now?" she asked.

"Gunnvald and I are testing sleds," Astrid explained, lifting her vehicle out of the snowdrift. "It's not dangerous."

"You think I believe that?" Sally exclaimed. "Just be careful you don't break your neck."

Astrid promised to do her best to avoid that. "Bye, Sally!"

27

* * *

"What a rubbish sled," Astrid complained once she was back up at the top with Gunnvald.

"What a rubbish driver," Gunnvald retorted.

"Teach me, then!" she shouted angrily.

So, as the sun approached Storr Peak, Gunnvald explained all he knew about the noble art of sled steering. He knew quite a lot.

A voice suddenly crackled out of the walkie-talkie. "Where's the test pilot? Over."

"She's in training!" Astrid yelled.

"Over," Gunnvald added.

Communications fell silent for a moment, but then: "Should I start the traffic again or what? Over."

"No way! Over and out," Gunnvald announced, plonking Astrid down onto the second sled, which was a shorter version of the first. "This one's better," he promised. "And so are you, now."

Astrid just had time to make a note of where the brake was before he gave her another massive push.

Hairy hedgehogs, this was something else! Astrid

suddenly had full control. The sled was obeying her orders just like that. When she reached the bridge, she braked elegantly, like Gunnvald had just taught her, and stopped herself from skidding. Sally had come all the way down to the road, and Astrid went past so fast that she made Sally's skirt flutter.

"Yoo-hoo, Sally. This is pretty dangerous!" Astrid shouted, leaning forward.

Onto the scrap heap with the toboggans! She was jet powered now! As she zoomed through the enchanted forest, she was showered with clumps of snow that couldn't cling to the trees anymore, but Astrid's sled drove straight on through them all. The words to a new sledding song came to her all by themselves:

> *"O-aaaah, here comes a sled a-rushing fast,*
> *O-aaaah, here comes a sled a-whizzing past."*

She was approaching Hagen's Wellness Retreat now, so she sang even more loudly.

> *"O-aaaah, it's going at a mile a minute.*
> *Make way, a sled in the middle of the rooo-ooad!"*

She caught a glimpse of Mr. Hagen between the

campsite reception and one of the cabins.

"In the middle, in the middle of the road—o-aaaah."

She went on singing as she sped by. Soon she spotted Peter in the distance.

"O-aaaah, here comes a sled a-braking,

O-aaaah, here comes a sled a-snaking."

With a beautiful skid that made the snow crystals dance in the last sunbeams of the day, Astrid Glimmerdal came to a halt one centimeter from Peter's black safety boots.

"Good afternoon," she said, getting up. Her legs ached from sitting in the same position for so long.

Peter ushered her carefully over to the bank of snow at the side of the road. There was a long line of cars behind him. They'd been stopped there since she started her first sled run. Which was some time ago.

"Luckily, I actually look like somebody doing roadwork," Peter said, nodding toward his digger. "They're all heading up to Hagen's Wellness Retreat."

Of course, it was Friday, Astrid remembered. She took a good look at each car. Old couples ready to go cross-country skiing as far as the eye could see. She sighed.

Just think: despite all the snow and sledding that Glimmerdal had to offer, there still wasn't a single child visiting on vacation. It was a disgrace.

When they were rattling back up the glen in Peter's brown Volvo, Astrid told him that Gunnvald thought they could make a sled that would run all the way down to the shoreline.

"He's already got one with really good runners," she explained as she watched the snowdrifts rushing past the window. Then she stopped and closed her mouth, because there was Mr. Hagen, in the middle of the road, looking like a deranged musk ox.

Peter slowed down and stopped. The car window's winding handle was broken, so he had to open the door. It hit Mr. Hagen in the stomach.

"What's this I hear about roadwork?" Mr. Hagen snarled. "My guests are saying they had to wait for an hour before they could get past."

Peter cleared his throat.

"Do you want me to report you to the police, you idiot?" Mr. Hagen shouted.

Astrid leaned forward in her seat. "You mustn't call people idiots," she scolded, giving Mr. Hagen her sternest look.

"You can when it's true!" Mr. Hagen shouted. "The same goes for you, Asny, and even more so. If I see you on that sled in the middle of the road one more time, I'm calling the police."

Before Astrid could say that her name wasn't Asny, Mr. Hagen stuck his flushed head into the car. "It's impossible to develop any proper tourism around here while you're on the loose! Did you know that? If I were your father, I wouldn't let you out!"

Astrid's eyes narrowed. What a horrible thing to say! "Mr. Hagen, you're a—"

Peter shut the door. "You mustn't call people idiots," he said nicely, stepping on it as they drove into the enchanted forest.

CHAPTER FOUR

In which Astrid doesn't worry about what Mr. Hagen says, and letters fall from the sky like snow

It's typical for people like Mr. Hagen to always ruin anything good or fun. Astrid was so worked up that she was pacing back and forth in Gunnvald's farmyard, waving her arms.

"And he still calls me Asny!" she shouted to finish, so that Gunnvald would see just how wrong it all was.

But Gunnvald merely huffed. "We shouldn't worry in the slightest about what that stick-in-the-mud says," he said simply. He invited Peter in for a cup of coffee to thank him for his good work.

But Astrid stayed sitting outside in a snowdrift, going

over and over what Mr. Hagen had said until her stomach hurt. Everything fun was bad for tourism! Even sledding. That lousy, wretched, swollen udder of a wellness camp. Shouldn't people be allowed to live in the glen too? She cast a sly glance at the three sleds. How dare Mr. Hagen call Peter an idiot! Peter was so good and kind that his eyes sparkled like lights. How dare Mr. Hagen say that her dad shouldn't let her out! And how dare he say that he'd report her to the police if she went sledding in the middle of the road again! Astrid was so angry that the snow boiled where she sat.

She could hear Gunnvald playing his fiddle in the kitchen. The notes filtered out through the door, dancing in the blue afternoon sky. The third sled, the one with the good runners, was gleaming, shining out at her, almost as if it were whispering, "Speed and self-confidence." When Gunnvald had told her that they shouldn't worry about what Mr. Hagen said, maybe he'd really meant that she should go for another sled run. Right down the middle of the road.

Astrid cast a quick glance over her shoulder and sat down tentatively on the unfinished sled. It didn't have brakes, but she'd barely needed to brake on the last run. She could use her legs. The sled was low and short, and it felt good sitting on it. She turned the steering wheel back and forth a couple times. It felt very good.

"Test pilot ready. Over and out," she muttered to herself, pushing off from the ice-covered farmyard before she had time to think twice.

When Astrid looked back on it afterward, what she remembered best was the feeling in her stomach just as she edged off down the slope. The little thunderbolt of Glimmerdal's curly hair was blown back along the sides of her helmet like racing stripes. When she crossed the bridge, she had to give it all she had to make the turn. Down by Sally's place, she brushed against the bank of snow but managed by the skin of her teeth to maneuver the sled back on track. She held on to the wheel as if her life depended on it. Actually, her life probably did depend on it right then. *Swoosh,* into the woods. *Ploff,* snow in her face. *F-shoom,* out of the woods. The air against her face made her eyes water.

"Ooooh!" cried Astrid, half-excited and half-scared.

Who would have thought it was possible to buffet and shake like that! Faster, faster, faster. Astrid was so gripped by her speed that she almost didn't notice she was approaching Hagen's Wellness Retreat. She even forgot to sing.

That was when she saw the mail truck. It was parked in the middle of the road next to the camp. Finn, the mailman, was running late that day; Astrid barely had time to reflect on this before she realized she needed to brake. The only thing was that she didn't have any brakes. She swung her feet to the ground and pushed her boots against the frozen road surface, scraping and rattling enough to make her teeth chatter. Surely she'd never manage to stop in time. Astrid was about to throw herself into the bank of snow when she saw that there was just enough space for a sled to squeeze past the mail truck. Her eyes narrowed. She pulled her legs back in tight and aimed the sled. Then Astrid Glimmerdal rode between the snowy shoulder and the truck with plenty of speed and self-confidence.

It would all have gone perfectly if it hadn't been for

Finn. Suddenly he appeared from behind the truck, carrying a whole box full of letters and newspapers.

"Look out!" Astrid screamed.

Finn threw his box up in the air and launched himself into the bank of snow, while Astrid Glimmerdal slid straight into a blizzard of bills and letters. An open copy of the local paper smacked into her face, covering her eyes and plunging her into darkness.

All good things come in threes. Once again she was flung into the deep snow, landing on her head. It's amazing how many times that can happen over the course of one Friday afternoon. Astrid quickly freed herself from the newspaper and struggled to her feet. Finn sat there, a mailman almost run over, his mail spread across half of Glimmerdal.

"Is that one of Gunnvald's new sleds?" he asked curiously.

Astrid's reply was drowned out by Mr. Hagen's yelling, which came rushing through the winter air like a hurricane. You'd have thought he was the one who had almost been run over.

"That's it, Asny, I've had it with you!"

Mr. Hagen was so angry that the snow melted beneath his feet. Astrid straightened her back and sighed, while Mr. Hagen's ranting filled the winter air.

Astrid didn't know then that she had just saved somebody. She knew nothing of the fact that Mr. Hagen had already been angry with another small person when he'd heard the racket by the gate. No, Astrid had no idea that there was a young boy standing behind one of the campsite cabins, watching with horror as Mr. Hagen hurled all of his rage at a red-haired girl with a sled instead of him. And the young boy behind the cabin, who was in fact so scared of Mr. Hagen that he thought he might die, was utterly astonished when he saw that the red-haired girl wasn't scared in the slightest. She calmly gathered up the letters and newspapers as if Mr. Hagen weren't there yelling at her.

There was one other thing Astrid didn't know. She didn't know that one of the letters she was picking up from the snow was the start of something that would change everything.

The small brown envelope was addressed to Gunnvald

Glimmerdal. And Gunnvald Glimmerdal was somebody Astrid knew very well.

"I can take this letter for you," she told Finn.

Then she saluted in her bike helmet like a miniature general and shuffled off back up the glen, pulling the sled behind her. But this time she didn't sing.

Even Astrid felt that enough was enough.

CHAPTER FIVE

In which Astrid, Dad, and Snorri the Seagull have dinner

There aren't many people who know about Glimmerdal. It's just there, hidden away—a bit of a secret. But not for Astrid, as it's where she's always lived. She knows all the rocks and the little nooks and crannies down by the river. She knows which trees are good for climbing, and she knows the name of every single one of the mountains that make a wreath around Glimmerdal. That evening, she stopped in the farmyard at home to look at the dark silhouettes of the mountaintops against the twilit sky.

Cairn Peak, that's the highest mountain. Some eagles have a nest on the steep slope close to the summit. Then there's the Glimmerhorn, which is where the sun sits at midday. Sometimes avalanches start from there in the winter. The Nape, that's the smaller mountain right behind Gunnvald's farm; it has a square patch of spruce forest on its belly, looking like an apron. Gunnvald's grandfather planted those trees with his own hands. And then there's Storr Peak, the dark mountain that casts its evening shadow over the glen.

"My mountains," Astrid murmured. "And my houses," she added when she turned and saw the two houses on the farm.

Astrid and her dad live in the new house, and so does Astrid's mom when she's home. Nobody lives in the old one. Astrid's uncles moved away before she was born and got married wherever it was they got married, and her grandparents moved back to her granny's hometown two years ago. They only really visit Glimmerdal in the summer now. But the lights are often on in the old house anyway, as Auntie Eira and Auntie Idun always stay there when they come home. Astrid and her dad sometimes stay there for a bit too, so that the old house doesn't feel totally neglected.

In the new house, in the light of the kitchen, Astrid could see her dad. He was puttering back and forth, probably making dinner. Snorri the Seagull sat on the coffeepot, watching him. It was Astrid's mom who had brought Snorri home when he was a little chick and had been trapped in a fishing net. He was almost dead when she found him out along the coast, so she took him home to Astrid and her dad. Snorri had spent a whole summer in Glimmerdal, and when his wing had healed, he hadn't wanted to leave. He was as happy as anything there beneath the mountains, even though he was a seagull.

"In that case, he can stay," Astrid had decided.

Snorri was given his own box in the hall and his own bowl in the kitchen. He was three years old now and had grown into a fat and noisy seagull of the worst kind. Astrid and her dad loved him. He got up to all sorts of things, and he reminded them of Astrid's mom. She must hear seagull cries all day long when she's working by the coast or out at sea, and that's where she often is. If you're going to learn things about the sea and oceans, then you have to be by the sea, otherwise it's no good. And if you're farmers in Glimmerdal, like Astrid and her dad, then you have to be in Glimmerdal, otherwise it's no good either. Astrid often wondered what on earth her mom and dad were thinking when they fell in love. They mustn't have been thinking at all.

At that moment, Astrid's mom was away in Greenland, finding out how much ice was melting. Astrid and her dad received e-mails from her almost every day, with pictures of all the things she was seeing and telling them about all her experiences.

"It's magnificent," she had written. "Greenland's absolutely magnificent."

Quite often, at night, Astrid dreamed that she was in Greenland. In one of her dreams, she was swimming among the ice floes with the seals, wearing only her swimsuit, but she wasn't cold. It was the most amazing dream she'd had in a long time.

Astrid opened the back door and stomped into the passageway along with a wintry gust of evening air.

"Hi, guys!" she shouted, startling both Snorri and her dad.

"I thought perhaps you'd decided never to come back," her dad said.

"I had to take a letter up to Gunnvald," Astrid explained, sitting down at the dinner table, which was already set.

"Why? Has something happened to Finn?"

"Almost," Astrid mumbled, thinking about what would have happened if she'd flattened him with the sled. "Gunnvald went all weird when I gave it to him. He turned it around and around, and looked at it as if he'd never seen a letter before." She chewed her food pensively, remembering the sight of Gunnvald with the brown envelope in his hands. It was as if he'd stopped breathing for a moment when he'd seen the return address.

"Who was it from?" Astrid's dad asked.

"I don't know; it was none of my beeswax."

They ate in silence for a while. Astrid's whole body was exhausted, but she felt good after her long afternoon out and about. Her toes stung and tingled.

"Mr. Hagen called," her dad said suddenly.

"We shouldn't worry about what Mr. Hagen says," Astrid replied quickly. "Gunnvald said so."

Her dad smiled behind his beard. "Well, if Gunnvald says so."

He gave Snorri a small ball of cheese. The cheese immediately got stuck in his beak, so he sat there with his mouth wide open, looking worse than a patient at the dentist.

Astrid laughed so hard that milk came out her nose.

CHAPTER SIX

In which Astrid sets out to find some disgusting snus, and ends up in a real fight

The next day, when Astrid and her dad had finished their Saturday-morning cleaning, she ran over to Gunnvald's to see how the sleds were coming along. But Gunnvald wasn't working on the sleds. He was in his kitchen, holding his fiddle and doing nothing.

"Are you just sitting there?" Astrid asked him, stomping out of her snow boots.

"Mmm-hmm," said Gunnvald.

Then Astrid saw something strange out the window: tracks in the snow leading up to the little summerhouse at the edge of the forest.

"Have you been in the summerhouse? What were you doing there?"

Gunnvald's grandfather had built the summerhouse more than a century ago, when he'd been abso-head-over-heels-lutely in love with a girl called Madelene Katrine Benedicte. Madelene Katrine Benedicte had a blue silk dress and fifty-two suitors, so Gunnvald had told Astrid. Gunnvald's grandfather was the fifty-third, but instead of giving her roses and rubbish like that, he'd built her a really good summerhouse.

"That has to be the most elaborate way of getting a girlfriend ever," Auntie Eira had said once. "Imagine if Peter took a leaf out of Gunnvald's grandfather's book and hammered together a summerhouse for you, Idun. Not bad, eh?"

Madelene Katrine Benedicte had never seen anything as beautiful as the little white house with its big windows. And she'd never met a more dashing man than Gunnvald's grandfather. That's how Gunnvald had ended up with the world's most beautiful grandmother and a summerhouse at the edge of the forest.

In summer, it's nice to sit in the summerhouse, playing cards and drinking fruity squash while thinking about Gunnvald's grandfather and the beautiful Madelene Katrine Benedicte. Gunnvald and Astrid often do that. But now it was winter. What on earth had Gunnvald been doing up there?

"You know that letter from yesterday?" Gunnvald said eventually, after Astrid had spent a good while badgering him.

"What about it?"

Gunnvald groaned. He seemed annoyed. "It was a letter saying that somebody I used to know has died."

Astrid took one of the homemade vanilla cookies from the bowl on the table. You wouldn't know from looking at Gunnvald that he was descended from a beautiful grandmother. His eyebrows resemble two worn-out toothbrushes.

"Who died?" she asked him.

"Nobody special."

"Nobody special?"

"No. Nobody special."

Gunnvald laid his fiddle on the table and pulled out

his snus tin. It was empty. "Oh, crab apples!" he shouted angrily, throwing the tin on the floor. Hulda was scared and leaped up into the kitchen sink.

Astrid knew only too well how grumpy Gunnvald got without that yucky snus of his. And now the shop was closed. That's what happens when you just sit there, thinking and not planning.

"I'll take the kick-sled and go down to Nils. He'll have a tin of snus you can borrow," she said. "You're impossible to be with when you're like this anyway."

Astrid went to find the kick-sled, an upright sled, a bit like a chair, that you can push around on the ice and snow. It's a good way to move fast without slipping. She jumped on the runners at the back, set off down the hill, and was soon whizzing past Hagen's Wellness Retreat.

"Gunnvald, he needs snus and bad,
And when he gets it he'll be glad.
Ralla-yalla-halla-yalla-yaaa!
But if he's grumpy as a goose,
There won't be any rotten snus:

49

I'll take his snus to Timbuktu.

Ralla-yalla-halla-yalla-yuuu!"

She looked like a snowman when she finally arrived at the bottom of the glen and parked outside the elder housing where Nils lives. Nils is Peter's grandfather. Every now and then he has what Peter calls a "funny turn." That's when Nils drinks too much beer. Nils's funny turns can last for a couple of days or they can last for several weeks. Even though Nils says a lot of strange and funny things when he has a funny turn, neither Peter nor Anna—Peter's grandmother—nor anybody else in Peter's family thinks it is any fun. Astrid wondered whether or not Nils would be having one of his turns that day. But most of all, she wondered whether or not he would have any snus.

Sure enough, he was having one of his turns. And he had some snus too.

"Anna, Ashtrid wantsh shome shnush!" Nils called out. Then he tottered off into the apartment.

Astrid stood waiting in the hall, and while she stood there, she heard the old couple having a strange conversation.

"Yes, Gunnvald probably needs some snus today," Anna whispered. "It said in one of the Oslo papers that Anna Zimmermann's died."

"Anna Zimmermann's died?" Nils shouted. "That old bag," he added.

"Shame on you, Nils!" Granny Anna scolded him. "You can't say things like that."

"I can say what I want about Anna Zimmermann. She was an old bag," Nils muttered. Then he came veering out into the hallway with the dreaded snus.

"Who's Anna Zimmermann?" Astrid asked.

"An old bag," said Nils, scratching under his nose. "Tell Gunnvald he can have this tin on me. He probably needs it."

Astrid's head was swimming as she pushed the kick-sled back up the glen. Anna Zimmermann? An old bag? Astrid had never heard of anybody named Anna Zimmermann in all her life. Was she the person Gunnvald had been thinking about in his summerhouse? Astrid was so deep in her thoughts that she passed Hagen's Wellness Retreat

51

without letting out a single verse of her latest song. It was only when she reached the enchanted forest that she saw something that almost made her eyes pop out on stalks.

There were two children walking along the road.

Astrid was so stunned that her mouth dropped open. Two boys! One of them was wearing camouflage pants and had a bandanna around his head. He was jumping about, kicking lumps of ice. The other was wearing normal clothes and walking peacefully along the shoulder. Could it really be true? Were there children on vacation in Glimmerdal?

The two boys caught sight of her and slowed down; soon they were all standing face-to-face in the middle of the snow-covered glen. Astrid was just about to smile when the boy with the bandanna opened his mouth.

"Don't mess with my brother."

Astrid raised her eyebrows.

"If you so much as touch my brother, I'll make mincemeat out of you and cook you with gravy," he warned, glaring at her threateningly.

The other boy, the one she wasn't supposed to touch, looked embarrassed.

Astrid couldn't stop herself. She put her kick-sled firmly to one side, then walked straight past the boy in the bandanna and up to his brother standing by the bank of snow. She poked him in the shoulder.

"You touched my brother!" the younger boy yelled.

Astrid smiled her broadest smile, but that was all she could manage before the little maniac threw himself at her like a lynx.

He was attacking her! In her own glen! Rabid ravens, did that make her angry.

"Aaaaaagh!" Astrid roared.

They grappled on the ice with such force that the snow poles marking the edges of the road trembled. He pulled Astrid's hair, pinched, grabbed, and hit her, and she did exactly the same back, at least as fiercely.

But suddenly the boy in the bandanna just stopped fighting. "Brother!" he shouted. Or at least that was what it sounded like. It was all so abrupt.

His brother was gone. Astrid couldn't believe it was possible to show so little interest in a real fight.

The younger boy ran off, shouting, "Brother, wait!

Brother!" His voice echoed in the mountains around Glimmerdal. How strange, Astrid thought. Why didn't he call his brother by his name? Slowly she brushed snow off herself. She was shivering, her hand hurt, and her head was pounding. What had just happened?

Then she noticed something that horrified her. The boy had taken the tin of snus.

Astrid accelerated her kick-sled to a dizzying speed and caught up with the brothers by Hagen's Wellness Retreat. She skidded to a halt, blocking the road ahead of them. She had learned that from Auntie Eira. It was easy to see that the two boys were brothers, even though one had dark hair and the other was blond. They both had the same bright spark in their eyes.

"The snus," said Astrid.

The younger boy with the straight dark hair was holding the tin in one hand, and he showed no sign of giving it up.

"Give me that revolting snus, please," Astrid said again. If only she knew how threatening she looked standing there, the little empress of Glimmerdal.

"Give her the snus, Ola." The boy Astrid wasn't

54

supposed to touch clearly could speak. He turned to her apologetically. "He doesn't mean it. He just—"

"You bet I mean it!" the smaller boy shouted, throwing the tin of snus as far as he could. It landed a bit farther up the road. "By the way, you fight like a girl," he snarled before storming off angrily into the camp.

"I *am* a girl!" Astrid yelled furiously after him.

The other boy was still there. The one she'd touched. He looked friendly, with his blond hair and bashful eyes. With all her heart, Astrid wished he would say something. Something nice. Her nose was bleeding, leaving red circles in the snow. But the boy didn't say anything. He simply looked down, then turned around and followed the snus thief.

Astrid was left standing alone outside the gate. "Idiots!"

Astrid's shouting made Mr. Hagen pull aside a curtain and shoot her a look that would have given most people the chills. But Astrid was only watching where the two brothers had disappeared behind the wall of a cabin.

"Idiots," she whispered, turning her kick-sled around.

CHAPTER SEVEN

In which Gunnvald tells Astrid about love, and Astrid tells Gunnvald about the teeny-tiniest billy goat Gruff

Back at Gunnvald's house, Astrid's tears began to flow. "I've been in a fight!" she sobbed.

An astonished Gunnvald pulled out Astrid's usual chair and found some tissues, while the little thunderbolt of Glimmerdal let the whole story come gushing forth. Gunnvald wondered if she had landed any good punches, and Astrid thought she had. He found some antiseptic and patched her up. While she sniffled on about how miserable life could be, Gunnvald made some hot chocolate out of real chocolate bars. He placed a steaming mug in front of Astrid, then took a big pinch of snus and put it under his lip. It was the most fantastic snus he'd ever tasted in all his seventy-four years, he said; you could almost tell that somebody had gone through fire and water to get hold of it. Glory to Nils and Astrid and all that was good in the world. Astrid would normally have said how absolutely revolting she thought snus was, but she was still too busy sniffling away. This was the most tragic thing that had ever happened to her. And she had longed so much for other children to come to Glimmerdal!

"Why do the first children who come here have to be such bullies?" she shouted.

"Calm down," said Gunnvald, hushing her. He got up and grabbed his fiddle. With the snus under his lip, he tucked his precious instrument under his chin and performed an entire concert just for Astrid.

Every once in a while, Liv, the church minister, would manage to cajole Gunnvald into playing in church. Astrid would usually go along. She would sit in the gallery watching Gunnvald, in his creased white shirt and his suit trousers that were too short, as he closed his eyes and sent his miraculous music floating out above the people

57

listening, up to the church rafters and all the way to heaven. Astrid felt so proud of Gunnvald then, but she thought it was almost just as nice listening to him play in the kitchen when it was only the two of them, Gunnvald wearing his woolen socks full of holes and with his hair all scruffy. Actually, it was almost better.

Astrid's dad had said that when Gunnvald was young, he used to play in a symphony orchestra in Oslo, but then he must have gotten tired of the whole symphony orchestra thing, because he moved home to Glimmerdal to take over the farm. Since then, Gunnvald had only played in the other villages in the area. Whenever Astrid went with Gunnvald to Barkvika or into town, people came over to him to talk about his fiddle music.

"Music's my heart," Gunnvald had once told Astrid. "Without my fiddle, I'd already be stone dead."

On days like this, Astrid knew what Gunnvald meant. It was as if the sound of his fiddle crept into her heart, making her feel a bit better. Then, at the end, just as Astrid always hoped he would, Gunnvald closed his eyes and drew the bow softly and carefully over the strings, filling his warm kitchen with the notes of an old goat-herding lullaby. The tune made Astrid start crying again, because it was the most beautiful she knew and so wonderfully sad that it made her stomach turn blue.

What did you need other children for when you had Gunnvald?

When the music had finished and Gunnvald had sat down, Astrid remembered something important that she'd forgotten in all the confusion.

"Who's Anna Zimmermann?"

Gunnvald looked as if he'd just had an electric shock. He gaped at Astrid, aghast. "How did, uh . . ." he spluttered. "Anna Zimmermann is dead."

"Yes, but who was she?"

Had it not been for the fight, and had Gunnvald not still been feeling a little sorry for Astrid, he might never have answered.

"Many, many years ago, Anna Zimmermann was my girlfriend."

It seemed to take all of Gunnvald's strength to say it.

"*You* had a girlfriend?"

Astrid looked at Gunnvald's shabby sweater, at his wild hair, and at the rest of him. Had *he* had a girlfriend? Yes, imagine that, he had, actually, he told her angrily.

"Is it lovesickness you've got, then?" she asked cautiously.

Astrid had great respect for lovesickness. She'd never had it herself, but her Auntie Eira had once. Auntie Eira's lovesickness was so bad that it had made the whole of the old house creak and groan. She'd stayed in bed for an entire week, refusing to get up until all the men in the world had died of the plague. If it was something similar that Gunnvald was suffering from, then that explained why he'd been sitting in the summerhouse in the middle of winter.

"Lovesickness, you little troll? Let's be very clear: I'm not lovesick," Gunnvald roared.

Still, something was wrong: that much was easy to see. And, if truth be told, Astrid was quite down herself.

"Okay, Gunnvald," she said, getting up from her chair. "You're going to go into the workshop and get started on the sleds again, and I'm going to cheer us up by telling the tale of the teeny-tiniest billy goat Gruff."

"The teeny-tiniest . . . ?" Gunnvald grunted irritably.

"Yes. Not many people have heard of the teeny-tiniest one. He never made his way into the normal version of the story," Astrid explained. "His brothers, the other three billy goats Gruff, left him before they reached the river and the troll."

"Oh?" Gunnvald muttered, getting up reluctantly.

"The other three billy goats were always mean to the teeny-tiniest one," Astrid said as they entered the workshop. "They bullied him because he was small, and they ignored him when he wanted to play. They even ate his food. That's why he was the teeny-tiniest one. Now he was really looking forward to reaching the hillside and making himself fat."

"Humph," said Gunnvald.

"But then they went off ahead of him, those stupid billy goats Gruff," Astrid continued. "When the teeny-tiniest billy goat finally got to the bridge, it was almost night. Under the bridge lay the troll, who wasn't feeling very well because the big billy goat Gruff had crushed him to bits, body and bones, as the story goes, when he'd tossed him out into the river earlier that day."

Yes, Gunnvald remembered that part, he grumbled as he turned one of the sleds upside down.

"But the special thing about trolls, which very few people know," Astrid said, "is that when someone's sad, and especially if they're small, then trolls are kinder than usual. Now, for example, the troll heard the teeny-tiniest billy goat Gruff's sad bleating and returned to his senses. 'Who's that crying on my bridge?' the troll asked cautiously.

"'It's only me, the teeny-tiniest billy goat Gruff, who would really like to go up to the hillside to get fat, but I'm so hungry that I don't have the strength,' said the teeny-tiniest billy goat Gruff, sinking to his knees. The troll knew only too well how the teeny-tiniest billy goat Gruff was feeling. The troll wasn't really bad; he was just very undernourished and lonely. That's usually the problem with trolls," she explained.

Gunnvald nodded.

"Then the troll said in his deep voice: 'Now I'm coming to—'

"'Yes, come on, then,' whimpered the teeny-tiniest billy goat Gruff, as he was so lonely too. Even though he was badly injured, the troll dragged himself up onto the bridge and sat down on the railing, which began to bend quite a bit. The teeny-tiniest billy goat Gruff used the last of his strength to jump up onto the railing too," said Astrid. "So there he was, in the middle of the bending bridge, listening to the troll, who was telling him about his awful meeting with the three billy goats Gruff and especially about how the biggest one had charged him and tossed him into the river. 'Did it hurt?' the teeny-tiniest billy goat Gruff asked him worriedly.

"'Did it hurt?' roared the troll. 'It hurt so much it gave the whole kingdom rheumatism!'"

Astrid took a break to think for a moment. Gunnvald wondered if the story had finished, and he looked up from the sled, but then she went on:

"The teeny-tiniest billy goat Gruff felt very sorry for the troll and said, 'When the three billy goats Gruff come home from the hillside, they'll all be twice as fat. Then you can eat them and be twice as full!' The troll thought this was a brilliant idea, yet the more he considered it, the more he realized that right now, just thinking about billy goats made his stomach ache. The troll decided he would rather have a chat instead, since now his troll heart was beating as warmly and kindly as it ever had, as he sat there with the teeny-tiniest billy goat Gruff."

"How's this going to end?" Gunnvald asked impatiently.

"Don't get me all stressed, you old duffer," said Astrid. "Otherwise it'll be a bad story. Anyway, when troll hearts beat long enough, then trolls become less and less troll-like and more and more like people. Eventually their hearts turn into completely normal human ones. If you absolutely must deal with a troll, it's much better to change it into a person than to crush it to bits, body and bones. This troll here, for example, spent so long sitting on the rail and having a nice chat with the teeny-tiniest billy goat Gruff that the troll was completely transformed into . . ."

Astrid paused for effect, giving Gunnvald a dramatic look.

". . . into a gigantic man with messy gray hair."

"Ha!" he shouted, pointing a menacing finger at her. "I know what you're getting at!"

Astrid chuckled with satisfaction as she sat there on the woodworking lathe.

"The gigantic man found himself a farm and a workshop at the top of a glen, not so far from the bridge and the river. Eventually, as the years went by, people forgot that he was really the troll from the story about the billy goats Gruff and thought he was a perfectly normal man. It's only when he plays the fiddle that they realize he must have grown up under Glimmerdal Bridge, because he plays so beautifully that the water kelpie must have taught him."

"Ha!" said Gunnvald again.

Astrid smiled. "And ickny-nacky-nory, that's the end of the story."

Gunnvald told her it was the most deranged fairy tale he'd ever heard, but then he turned all serious and stared out the window.

"How did you know I'm really a troll, Astrid?"

"You aren't a troll anymore. You *used* to be a troll," she corrected him. "There's a big difference."

When Astrid went to bed that evening, a lone light could be seen shining out from Gunnvald's summerhouse. Fiddle music came trickling down across the glen. It sounded so beautiful and sad that it made her feel quite strange.

Very solemnly she put her hands together. "Dear God, please take care of everybody who's lovesick, especially Gunnvald, because now he's playing his fiddle in the summerhouse in the middle of winter. Amen. And, by the way," she added, "those boys . . . *Pfft,* no, just forget it; I couldn't care less about them. Amen."

Then Astrid lay down, but she didn't fall asleep. It was impossible to sleep after days like this when everything had been turned upside down.

People were awake throughout Glimmerdal that night. Over in the summerhouse, an old troll was playing his fiddle because he'd received a letter. Across the river from him lay Astrid, with her lion's mane of curls, listening and thinking about the fight and the boys and Anna Zimmermann. Meanwhile, down at Hagen's Wellness Retreat, far away from the music, two young boys lay awake, staring at the ceiling.

Astrid had no way of knowing that the brothers had actually been there in the road because they'd gone out especially to look for her. She had no way of knowing that a young boy was lying in his bed down at Hagen's Wellness Retreat, biting back tears because, for some compulsive reason or another, he couldn't help fighting people when he really only meant to say hello. Neither did she have any way of knowing that, luckily, the boy in the other bed was trying to cheer him up by telling him that, in spite of everything, it had been quite a short and well-mannered fight, and that life was full of ups and downs, even if things had mostly been down recently.

There are so many things we have no way of knowing, unfortunately. That's just the way things are.

CHAPTER EIGHT
In which Astrid makes three new friends

The next morning, Astrid was pacing around the living room in circles, with Snorri the Seagull hot on her heels.

"Go and look for them," her dad said after a while.

Astrid paced around a little longer before suddenly breaking off and stomping outside.

She could go skiing. She could jump from the Little Hammer. She could follow the fresh fox tracks in the field. She could go and see Gunnvald. Astrid's whole Sunday was free and empty, and she could do whatever she wanted; but all she could think about were the two boys down at Hagen's Wellness Retreat. Even though she didn't want to think about them. She didn't like spending time thinking about anyone who attacked innocent people for no reason.

"I couldn't care less about them!" she shouted up at the sky, sending the nearest falling snowflakes swirling back up toward the clouds.

It was just that it was absolutely impossible not to think about them. What in heaven's name were they doing down at that vacation camp anyway? Children weren't allowed there.

"Oh, good grief," Astrid said eventually. She set off past Sally's house, through the enchanted forest, and all the way down to the vacation camp.

She stopped outside the gate and saw them right away. The boy she wasn't supposed to touch was standing beneath the whirligig washing line, and the younger boy was swinging as he dangled from one of its metal bars. Before Astrid even knew what she was doing, she'd rolled a snowball and sent it flying. It hit its target, and the boy fell to the ground like a sack of potatoes. He leaped back up, furious, but when he saw who it was, he stopped dead.

There they stood, the three of them: Astrid, the younger

69

boy, and the one she wasn't supposed to touch. It was as if time stood still for a moment.

"If you'd swung there much longer," Astrid said eventually, "Mr. Hagen would've clipped clothespins on you, and you'd have been left dangling forever."

The boy cautiously approached. Soon he was standing by the gate. His hair was sleek and brown under his bandanna.

"My name's Astrid," said Astrid.

The boy drew a breath. Then he looked straight at her with his brown eyes and told her his name was Ola. "I'm eight years old. That's Broder over there. He's ten." He nodded to the other boy, who was still standing under the washing line.

"What's his name?" Astrid asked.

"Broder. His name's Broder."

"I thought you were saying 'Brother.' What kind of a name is that?"

"A Danish one," Ola barked.

"Why doesn't he come over here?"

"He's looking after Birgitte."

Then Astrid noticed a pink woolly hat sticking out of the snow a short distance away from the boy she now

70

knew was called Broder. A little sister? Astrid's heart
did a somersault. There were so many things in life she
wanted—an accordion, some rabbits, her own chain saw,
and some new twin-tip skis like her aunts had. She wanted
Auntie Idun and Peter to get together, wellness retreats to be
banned, and peace on Earth. She wanted a rope swing over
the swimming hole by the bridge at the mountain pasture,
a four-poster bed like her classmate Andrea had, and she
wanted the ice in Greenland to stop melting so her mom
wouldn't be so busy. But more than any of that, more than
anything in the whole world, Astrid wanted a little sister.

"What good would a little sister be to you?" Gunnvald
had asked her once.

"I'd teach her."

"Teach her how to get into trouble?"

"Yup, that too."

Astrid, who had been forbidden from setting foot
in Hagen's Wellness Retreat, slipped through the gate
undaunted. She walked straight up to the boy under the
washing line and smiled at little Birgitte in the snow. She
was a tiny round thing and couldn't have been more than

three years old. Astrid reached out a hand to the boy looking after her.

"My name's Astrid."

"Broder," said the boy, shaking her hand warily.

He looked friendly, this big brother. His blond hair was slightly curly, reminding Astrid of a picture of one of the angels in Sally's old Bible.

"Welcome to Glimmerdal," Astrid announced in her unique way.

Just as she was saying it, Mr. Hagen came around the corner of one of the cabins.

Auntie Eira had once told Astrid that if she ever met a bear, she should lie down and play dead. Then the bear would leave her alone. Before the other children could draw breath, Astrid swan-dived into the fresh snow.

Mr. Hagen let out a roar. "Asny!"

Astrid lay in the snow, playing dead with all her might, even though she very much wanted to turn around and yell at him once and for all that her name was Astrid, not Asny, and if he called her the wrong name one more time, she would really go berserk. But she played dead. She even held her breath. Nobody can do anything wrong when they're dead. Not even Astrid Glimmerdal.

"Get out of here, Asny."

He was right above her. Astrid would have preferred to encounter a bear, if she were honest. Luckily, just then somebody rang the bell in reception, so Mr. Hagen had to go.

"Get out of here!" he warned her as he left. "There are too many of you as it is!"

Astrid lay still until Birgitte poked her with a plastic shovel and said, "Good morning." Then she rolled over and smiled.

"Do you want to come and meet Gunnvald?"

"Yes," said Birgitte, who didn't know who Gunnvald was, but surely anywhere was better than Hagen's Wellness Retreat, with that angry man. Broder popped into one of the cabins to say where they were going, and then Astrid led the whole gang out through the gate to safety.

Broder walked in the middle, holding Birgitte's hand. Ola threw snowballs and jumped up onto the banks of snow.

"Is that man mad at you?" Broder asked.

"You could say that, yes," Astrid admitted.

"I think he's mad at us too. Why is he so angry?"

"He'd prefer us to stay indoors until we've grown out of being children," Astrid explained. "But we shouldn't worry about what he says," she added, as sure of those words as if Gunnvald himself had just said them.

"Are you two mortal enemies?" Ola asked from the snowbank just above them, bending back a snow pole, then letting it go with a terrific *twang*.

Astrid had to think about it for a moment. "I don't know about mortal enemies," she said. That might be taking it a bit far. Then she was struck by a terrible thought. "You're not related to Mr. Hagen, are you? If you're allowed to stay at the camp?"

"Related to him? No! Are you totally deranged?" Ola shouted.

"Mom was going to come here for one of those wellness breaks, and we were supposed to go to our dad's place in Denmark," Broder explained.

"We used to live there when Mom and Dad were still married," Ola added.

"Demmak," said Birgitte.

"But then Dad said it wasn't convenient for us to visit after all," Broder mumbled. "It was a bit of a drama. Mom had to arrange for us to come here with her, even though it's not allowed. We have to be as good as gold."

"And we're doing our *veeeeery* best," shouted Ola, practically singing the word "veeeeery" in a high-pitched voice. Then he stopped, his eyes wide. "Astrid, there's a lady spying on us!"

Before Astrid could stop him, Ola had made a snowball and sent it flying at top speed toward Sally's windowpane. It struck, and Astrid saw Sally's perm drop behind her potted plant.

Sally was just getting up from the floor when Astrid came rushing in, Ola hot on her heels.

"Are you alive?" Astrid asked worriedly, stomping across the floor without taking off her boots, tracking snow all over the carpet.

"Who's that with you?" Sally asked weakly, as Astrid picked up her glasses and put them back on her face.

"His name's Ola. He thought you were some kind of

spy," said Astrid. "Actually, come to think of it, I suppose that's what you are."

Sally said hello to Ola, and he obligingly answered all of her questions. He told her that he came from town, he lived in a block of apartments, and he'd recently turned eight. Sally kept on asking questions.

"There are another two out in the snow," Astrid explained, "so we'll have to get going."

"Do you want some squash to drink?" Sally asked them.

Astrid shook her head. Auntie Eira once told her that only a very generous person would say that Sally's squash was squash at all. It looks more like water that something suspect has happened to, or at least that's what Auntie Eira thinks. But really Sally's squash is all right, maybe just a little weak. It's more that Gunnvald's squash is so good it's ungodly, as Auntie Idun says.

Astrid usually hangs around with Gunnvald in his kitchen toward the end of the summer when he has his big squash-making extravaganzas. He boils and strains the fruit, tastes it and smacks his lips, and then conjures up bottle after bottle of bilberry squash, black-currant squash, his secret unsweetened crowberry cordial, and Astrid's favorite squash, which is made out of raspberries and sun-ripened red currants. Actually, Astrid thinks the best thing about Gunnvald's squash-making extravaganzas is the pulp he scoops out of his bubbling pots of berries. It's really supposed to be thrown away, but Astrid spreads it on slices of bread, stuffing it all down until her stomach's like a beach ball. Sitting perched on Gunnvald's kitchen counter, eating bread with lukewarm pink pulp on top while the whole house smells of berries is practically heaven.

"We'll have squash at Gunnvald's place," Astrid whispered to Ola as she dragged him away.

Gunnvald was just coming out of the barn when the small procession appeared in his farmyard.

"Look what I found!" Astrid announced, gesturing at her three guests like a circus ringmaster.

"Which one of you mowed Astrid down yesterday?" Gunnvald thundered, the earflaps on his hat fluttering like flags in the wind.

Ola took a step back. "I did," he said softly.

"Do you normally mow down people you've just met?" Gunnvald asked him.

"Yes . . ."

"But he doesn't do it on purpose," his curly-haired brother quickly added.

"All we mow down here in Glimmerdal is the grass," said Gunnvald. He'd been waiting for Astrid, he added, as he had a marble cake baking in the oven.

Ola, Broder, and Birgitte had never tried marble cake before. They hadn't thought huge men like Gunnvald baked cakes either. At first they sat quietly around Gunnvald's enormous kitchen table, eating cake and drinking squash.

"Maaaaw?" said Birgitte when she'd finished, pushing her empty plate across the table.

Ola wriggled in his chair, and then he got up and ran off through the many rooms in Gunnvald's house.

"Sugar gives him a lot of energy," Broder explained as they listened to Ola running through the house. "Mom says we should get him a hamster wheel. That was a very tasty cake, by the way."

"Energy?" said Gunnvald.

As he gulped down the last swig of his coffee, Astrid knew this meant it was time to do some more sled testing in Glimmerdal.

CHAPTER NINE

In which Sled Test Run No. 2 is launched, and Gunnvald makes venison stew

It's a good thing Astrid showed up at Hagen's Wellness Retreat that day. It wasn't easy being a child there, as the others had been finding out. Ola, the restless one, had been trying so hard to be seen and not heard that he practically had smoke coming out of his ears. He was the one who'd been getting told off by Mr. Hagen on Friday when Astrid drove her sled into Finn's cloud of letters. Birgitte had been spending the whole time whining and upset. Broder, meanwhile, had been feeling anxious in the way only a big brother with curly blond hair and kind eyes can.

Ola and Broder didn't quite know how it had happened,

but each boy now suddenly found himself sitting on his own steerable sled, preparing for a test run as if they were two ordinary children on an ordinary winter vacation. Astrid had even been home to fetch Auntie Eira's and Auntie Idun's moped helmets for them. They looked like Formula One drivers.

"Speed and self-confidence, they're the key," the little thunderbolt of Glimmerdal explained, rubbing her mittens together.

What a day it turned out to be! A day of laughter and shouting. Gunnvald had made even more prototype sleds, and the mountains smiled at one another as they threw screams and shouts back and forth between them all the way down the glen. Astrid sang her sledding song at the top of her voice almost nonstop, and it wasn't long before Ola and Broder joined in. Especially Ola, who was a great singer. He could really make some noise. Birgitte stood next to Gunnvald, shouting "Go, go!" as loud as she could. They raced each other one on one; they crashed; they tipped over; they flew out into the snow; they got wet bottoms and red cheeks. They swapped sleds, comparing notes, getting rides in Peter's car, giving reports to Gunnvald. They tightened their helmets and did it all over again. At one point, Ola and Astrid collided, sending Ola flying all the way up into the second branch of a spruce tree by the side of the road. Another time it was Broder who flew headfirst into a ditch, landing on some dog mess. Astrid thought she would die laughing. And poor Sally! Her lunch went cold before she had a chance to eat it. She kept having to dash to her living-room window to watch them speed past on their sleds.

But when the sun descended behind Storr Peak, things quieted down. They were absolutely worn out.

"All troops return to base. Over," Gunnvald commanded. He'd promised to make venison stew for the whole gang, and that was a good thing too, as they were as famished as young hyenas.

Every autumn, Auntie Eira and Auntie Idun come home to join in the deer hunt. Astrid thinks deer hunting is like an adventure: scary and exciting at the same time. Last year, she'd been handed down some old camouflage gear and been allowed to sit under Auntie Idun's secret hunting tree.

"Now, you've got to be quiet," Auntie Idun had said.

Auntie Idun telling you to be quiet is quite different from Mr. Hagen telling you. Astrid sat there under the tree with Auntie Idun for three hours without saying a single word. They listened to the river rushing by and the trees whispering. The branches around them were decked in fiery red and gold. The air was as clear as can be, beneath a light blue autumn sky. Astrid remembers those hours spent with Auntie Idun as some of the best in her life. Auntie Idun sat with her gun over her leg while she kept watch. Every now and then, she looked at Astrid and smiled. Astrid started wishing she had a little sister again, one she could be kind to, one she could take along to a tree and wait with for the deer to come.

Eventually one emerged from the forest. A tall, handsome stag, strolling peacefully out into the clearing. Astrid still remembers how she stopped breathing while Auntie Idun took aim and fired. It happened so quickly that she almost didn't realize what was going on. The shot was the loudest thing she had ever heard, and the stag died instantly.

"He's four years old. Can you see?" said Auntie Idun, showing Astrid how you could tell from the antlers.

Astrid stroked the deer while Auntie Idun took out her knife. Just imagine, that guy had been running around Glimmerdal Forest all his life. Maybe he had fawns. For a moment, Astrid felt sad. But then Auntie Eira came crashing through the undergrowth, more or less the same way the deer had come.

"Wow-ee! That's our Sunday dinners at Gunnvald's for the next hundred years," she shouted.

Gunnvald makes such good venison stew that rumors of it reach as far as Barkvika. While Peter drank coffee by the window and Birgitte fell asleep on the sofa, Gunnvald browned the venison with some butter in a large pan. Astrid fetched the can of juniper berries and let Ola crush some with a rolling pin. They mixed the crushed berries with some pepper and sprinkled the mixture all over the sizzling meat. The smell was so good that Ola thought it might drive him crazy. It was almost unbearable standing there smelling the food without being able to eat it. Gunnvald let Ola chop up a head of lettuce with the kitchen knife while he was waiting. It could be turned into some kind of salad when he'd finished. Broder measured out the rice. Then Gunnvald put the venison on a plate and started to make some sauce. Onions, stock, cream, mushrooms that Astrid's mom had picked for him last autumn, a piece of traditional Norwegian brown cheese, lingonberry jam, salt, and a little water. Gunnvald mixed it, tasted it, and made an odd grunting noise now and then, as he usually does when he cooks.

Suddenly Ola said, "Our dad knows how to make venison stew too."

"Oh?" Gunnvald tipped the meat into the sauce without letting a single bit fall out of the pot.

"No, he doesn't," said Broder, on the other side of Gunnvald.

"Yes, he does!" Ola shouted stubbornly.

"Dad doesn't know how to make venison stew, Ola. Dad's a twerp." Broder's voice took on a harsh tone.

"You take that back!" Ola yelled.

But Broder wasn't about to take anything back. "Dad *is* a twerp. He doesn't know how to make venison stew; he never calls; he's—"

"He called on my birthday!" Ola's face was so red it looked like he was about to explode.

"It's been a whole month since your birthday!" Broder was shouting now too. "He doesn't care about us anymore! If he cared about us, we wouldn't be down at that stupid camp. We'd be in Denmark! But he always says it's not convenient; he never visits us; he never writes; he—"

It was as if Ola and Broder didn't even notice that there were still other people in the kitchen.

Ola took a ladle and threw it at the wall, splattering sauce everywhere. "You're a complete moron!" he shouted, running out into the wintry weather. The door slammed shut behind him, shaking the whole house.

Astrid sat on the kitchen counter, waiting for Gunnvald to sort it all out. But Gunnvald just stood there as if he'd turned to stone.

"Sorry," Broder said softly.

Wasn't Gunnvald going to say something? Wasn't

Gunnvald going to reassure Broder and tell him it was all right, then fetch Ola and straighten everything out? Astrid sat on the counter for a little longer before realizing that Gunnvald wasn't going to do anything.

It was Astrid who had to comfort Broder, and Peter who had to go out into the barn and find Ola behind some sacks of wool. Birgitte woke up and got everybody smiling again when she said, "Good morning." Gunnvald, on the other hand, didn't say a word. He just finished making the stew and served it.

Gunnvald didn't say anything while they were eating, either. It was as quiet as if they were far up on the mountain plateau. Birgitte was the only one talking.

"You help?" she said to Peter, getting him to cut the venison on her plate into smaller pieces.

Every now and then, Astrid glanced over at the two red-eyed brothers with a twerp for a father, and then at Gunnvald, who had suddenly gone all silent. When everyone's plates were empty, it was still quiet, so Astrid climbed up on the sofa and fetched Gunnvald's fiddle down from the wall. She plonked it in his lap. Then she

87

stood on her chair and started singing the first verse of
the old goat-herding lullaby in the heartfelt way that only
Astrid could sing:

> *"Bluey, billy goat of mine,*
> *Please tonight give me a sign,*
> *Or the bristly bear just might*
> *Come and capture you tonight."*

Astrid's singing carried through the walls, floating out
into the wintry Glimmerdal air.

> *"Old Lucky, your mother true,*
> *Came home late looking for you.*
> *Her bell ringing 'round about,*
> *Danger, fear, there seemed no doubt."*

A smallish lady was, at that very moment, coming up
through the farmyard in the evening gloom, and she recognized the voice. She'd heard it all day from the vacation
camp. Cautiously she climbed up the big stone steps to
Gunnvald's house. She raised a hand to knock on the door,
but then the fiddle finally joined in at the third verse:

> *"Has the bear on you then fed?*
> *Are you lying out there dead?*

You used to dance here and there,
While I shared my every care."

The lady stood there, her hand poised to knock, while Astrid sang the next verses about how much the goatherd loved Bluey, and how much Bluey loved the goatherd, and while the notes from Gunnvald's fiddle wrapped warmly around the words. The lady had never heard anything so beautiful, and the very same thing happened to her as happens to everybody when Gunnvald plays his fiddle. She fell completely still. Astrid had come to the last verse, which she always sings a little out of tune, because it's so sad.

"Bluey, Bluey, let us meet;
Let me hear your friendly bleat!
Don't die yet, oh, goat of mine.
Don't leave me to mourn and pine."

"What a beautiful song," the lady said once the music had finished.

They hadn't noticed her come into the kitchen. In fact, Gunnvald, Astrid, and Peter had never seen her before. But Ola, Broder, and Birgitte had.

"Mom!" Ola shouted happily. "We made venison stew!"

Every now and then you meet a person whom you like right away. This mom was like that. She had kind eyes, and even though she looked tired and worn out, her smile warmed the whole kitchen. Ola and Broder told her all about the sledding, both of them talking at exactly the same time. Peter found an extra chair, and Gunnvald scooped some more venison stew out of the pot for the new guest. Astrid suddenly missed her own mother so much that her stomach hurt. She almost wanted to go and sit right up close to this lady with the kind eyes whom she'd never seen before, just to see what it felt like. But she settled for smiling at her from the other side of the table.

It was a golden evening. Gunnvald opened the door to one of the many sitting rooms in his house and lit the fire. In Gunnvald's workshop, Astrid found the giant ludo board that she'd started making with Gunnvald the year before but never quite finished. She laid out the board tiles on the floor and found the counters, which were the size of dinner plates. Gunnvald played some more on his fiddle, and it was nighttime before they knew it. Eventually everybody shook

Gunnvald's gigantic hand to thank him for the dinner, and for the music, and then Peter drove the little family back down the glen.

It was quiet when they'd all left. Astrid started putting on her outdoor gear. She turned to Gunnvald. "Imagine having a father who only calls when it's your birthday." She pulled her hat low over her lion curls. The very thought made her angry. "We'll have to make sure their vacation here is the best ever, Gunnvald," she said as she opened the door.

Gunnvald didn't answer, and she glanced around. He just stood there, looking out the dark kitchen window.

"Gunnvald?"

"Mmm?"

"It's a good thing you've got me."

When Astrid had left, Gunnvald stood for a long time in the dimly lit kitchen. He could still hear the harsh, hurt tone in Broder's voice when he'd spoken about his father never calling and never writing. Deep inside his troll's heart, Gunnvald wondered what that dad in Denmark, whom he'd never met, could be thinking. After a while, he plodded over to the bookshelf and pulled out a small brown envelope. It was the letter.

Gunnvald had already read it so many times that it was frayed at the edges. Now he read it again. He hadn't written a reply. He never wrote letters.

CHAPTER TEN

In which Mr. Hagen goes too far, and the famous story "Do You Remember When Astrid Glimmerdal Drove Her Sled onto the Ferry?" is born

There are many stories about the girls of Glimmerdal. Not least about Auntie Eira and Auntie Idun. But Oskar Glimmerdal, Astrid's grandpa, isn't so keen on these stories. Astrid's grandpa is a very strict and proper man, being a retired school principal and all. He doesn't like it one bit when people in the shop tell stories about his daughters. But people still do. For example, they say, "Do you remember when Oskar's twins paddled down the river in a bathtub?" Then they roar with laughter. The story of Auntie Eira and Auntie Idun's voyage in a bathtub is definitely the best known, but there are many other stories about the girls of Glimmerdal. Most of them have been about Astrid since her aunts moved away.

That Monday, when the little thunderbolt of Glimmerdal got up, she had no idea it would be such a historic day. If people knew things like that in advance, there wouldn't be many stories worth telling.

"I'm going down to the vacation camp!" she called to her dad.

The air was a little less cold that morning. It was perfect snowball weather. Astrid pushed off from the bottom step outside the house, sending herself skating right across the hard-packed ice in the farmyard. The ice was beginning to melt under the sun's rays, with water gurgling and dripping everywhere. Astrid filled her lungs with the scent of spruce and squinted at the sun. She called days like this "diamond days." She hummed as she walked through the enchanted forest. It was so slippery underfoot that she almost fell several times. Sally would have to be careful not to break her leg!

But the slippery surface ended outside Hagen's Wellness Retreat. Mr. Hagen had spread grit all over the road outside the camp. It was icy again just beyond there, but it would be impossible to ride a sled down the stretch with the grit on it.

"He might at least have left a small gap." She sighed. But she was in too good a mood to feel angry. Soon she'd be seeing her friends!

She stopped by the gate. A lady wellness camper was there, getting her skis ready.

"Are you looking for the children?"

Astrid nodded.

"They're gone," the lady said. "They left a short while ago."

"But . . ." Astrid was stunned. "They didn't say anything yesterday about leaving."

The lady smiled sympathetically. "I don't think they wanted to leave."

Astrid leaned a little to one side so she could see past the lady and into the camp. Mr. Hagen was at the reception window. When Astrid spotted him, he turned away. Surely not! She opened the gate with a clatter. Soon she was standing face-to-face with Mr. Hagen. Or, more accurately, face-to-stomach with Mr. Hagen, since Astrid was quite small compared to him.

"Are you here to complain about the grit on the road?" he asked. If only he knew how little Astrid Glimmerdal cared about that grit of his.

"Have you kicked them out?"

Astrid's voice was so hurt that Mr. Hagen looked down busily at his papers.

"Children aren't allowed here. I gave them one chance, and they thoroughly abused it," he blustered. "You were making a terrible racket the whole day yesterday with that sledding of yours! It was unbearable."

Mr. Hagen was probably expecting Astrid to explode, to shout at him or throw things on the floor, or do something else that would give him an excuse to get angry with her. But Astrid didn't shout or throw anything. She did something even worse. She did nothing.

Mr. Hagen had to stand there and watch as Astrid Glimmerdal turned around and trudged out of reception. Then Mr. Hagen had to watch through the window as she wiped her eyes with her mitten and the kind lady with the skis stroked her face. Finally he had to watch as Astrid walked out through the gate and trudged back up Glimmerdal Road with her head bowed. Instead of the angry child he'd been expecting, Mr. Hagen saw a heartbroken one, and that was enough to move even him. Especially on that day, when he'd already seen quite a few heartbroken children. He suddenly felt like a real lowlife as he stood there by the window.

It was no longer a diamond day. Astrid walked back through the enchanted forest, fighting tears. When she reached Gunnvald's place, she saw that his garage was empty. He was probably down at the shop, buying some snus. Astrid kicked the snow off her boots and went into the kitchen. She stood in the middle of the room, wondering what she should do now. It was so quiet that she could hear Gunnvald's homemade clock ticking. It was a quarter to eleven. She sat down in the rocking chair and rocked back and forth. Now it was fourteen minutes to eleven. Astrid leaped out of the chair as abruptly as if she'd sat on a tack. Fourteen minutes to eleven! That meant there were fourteen minutes until the boat left. That meant that Ola, Broder, Birgitte, and their mom were still down at the ferry landing. Suddenly Astrid knew she had to go and say good-bye.

But fourteen minutes! She needed a car. Where could she get one if Gunnvald wasn't here?

"Dad!"

But no, even if her dad would drive her, they'd never make it in fourteen minutes if she had to run all the way home first. Before Astrid could finish that thought, she'd already dashed into the workshop and fetched the super-duper sled—the one with the best runners.

And that's when the famous story began.

Because Astrid Glimmerdal managed to get the sled going flat-out that morning. She went like lightning down the slope toward the bridge over the river. After all the testing, she'd become a skilled sledder, but that wasn't the only thing: the runners were freshly polished, the road was as slippery as soap, and the pilot was fearless. Astrid went so fast that not even Sally spotted the dark shadow zooming past her house and into the enchanted forest at eleven minutes to eleven, making an almost supernatural *shwoom*.

Astrid couldn't hear anything except the wind and couldn't feel anything except the sled shaking. And it was only when she saw the camp that she remembered this sled was still missing brakes. Her hands started to sweat, in spite of the cold air. What about the grit? She was going to get badly injured!

She didn't really know why she didn't try to stop. It could all end very badly, but she still leaned forward, eyes narrowed. Speed and self-confidence. The sled was now going even faster. The gritted stretch of road was coming toward her, right in her path. Astrid tilted hard to the left and felt the sled tip onto one runner. She steered the other runner up onto the bank of snow at the side of the road. There was a terrible jolt when metal hit grit, but because Astrid was practically lying horizontally, only one of the runners bore the brunt. She sped past the grit and came back down onto the road with a thump. She'd done it!

Still racing at a good speed, she flew past the place where Peter usually stood with his walkie-talkie. From then on,

Astrid and the super-sled were in uncharted territory. She came to a gradual incline: a long uphill slope that nobody had ever managed to climb on a sled before. Astrid had no idea what time it was. She leaned even farther forward, her eyes half-open. She was slowing down.

"Come on!" she whispered. "I've got to catch the boat!"

She could see the top of the hill. It seemed impossible, but perhaps she was going to make it. Astrid willed the sled up the hill. And, believe it or not, just before the sled came to a complete stop, Astrid Glimmerdal edged over the brow of the hill and sped up again.

Now she was down by the other houses, and it was high time to stop, but Astrid still needed to reach the water! She sped past Theo's hair salon, past the shop and the closed-down snack bar. Then, finally: there was the ferry ramp.

It was as if something went *click* in Astrid's head, bringing her to her senses. *Brake!* The little thunderbolt of Glimmerdal dug both heels into the ground. But it was too late. She skidded toward the ramp at one heck of a speed.

The only child in Glimmerdal realized that she would

have to throw herself off the sled, otherwise Glimmerdal would end up with no children at all. But then, to her horror, she noticed that one of the straps on her jacket had wound itself around the steering column. She was stuck! Astrid pushed her feet even harder into the ground. She was almost down at the fjord. If she didn't stop or overturn the sled soon, there was only the ice-cold water of the Glimmerdal Fjord left.

"Heeeeeeeeeeeeelp!" Astrid shouted, her whole body shaking and rattling. Her boots scraped against the uneven surface, leaving a smell of burnt rubber. She was going to end up in the water!

Then Astrid suddenly realized what might just save her. The high-speed ferry always docked bow first, with its wide ramp down to let passengers on and off. It was half a minute to eleven, and the crew hadn't raised the gangway yet.

Astrid turned the steering wheel hard. "Make way!" she shouted to the passengers who were boarding.

They jumped to the sides. The ice beneath the sled turned to metal. Skidding, scraping, her eyes shut, Astrid

Glimmerdal slid up the gangway in an almighty shower of sparks. The horde of passengers watched the sled and the girl in terror.

Then everything went completely silent. Astrid's heart was running like a hamster in her chest.

"Phew!" was all she managed to say.

There was a real commotion at the wharf that Monday morning when people found out that the little thunderbolt of Glimmerdal had driven one of Gunnvald's new sleds all the way down to the water's edge. Theo, the hairdresser, abandoned a perm he was doing; Able Seaman Jon took off his ticket bag; and the ferry passengers wanted to hear all about it. Even Nils, who was out for a stroll with his walker, staggered down to the gangway. But Ola, Broder, Birgitte, and their mom stood a little to one side with all their bags, ready to go, so Astrid let sleds be sleds and went over to them.

"I don't think Hagen's Wellness Retreat is the place for us," the children's mom said when she saw the despair in the sled pilot's eyes. Astrid had just opened her mouth to protest, when suddenly she heard Gunnvald's booming voice behind her. He'd just arrived from the shop.

"What's going on here?" he asked.

"Astrid rode her sled all the way down to the fjord!" Ola shouted.

Gunnvald lifted Astrid up by the tops of her arms, swinging her into the air so he could look her straight in the eye. "Is this true?" he asked.

Astrid nodded as she dangled there.

"But my dear little troll, my brave test pilot, why aren't you smiling?" he asked. Then he saw the little family had their bags with them.

It's hard to know exactly what Gunnvald would've said to Klaus Hagen if he'd been there at that very moment, but it wouldn't have been anything nice, that's for sure.

"That snake has gone too far this time," he muttered. Then he looked straight at Astrid. "You mustn't be upset on a day like this, Astrid. Blooming brambles, we can jolly well start our own wellness camp."

So that's how Gunnvald ended up inviting the little family to stay with him for the rest of their vacation. Free of charge. There were seventeen unused rooms in his house, he said, and Astrid knew that was true. Gunnvald's grandfather hadn't stopped with the summerhouse. He'd hammered and bashed and carpentered away for the beautiful Madelene Katrine Benedicte all his life. Eventually their house was as large as a hotel.

"There's heaps of space," Astrid agreed.

Of course, it took some persuading to convince Ola, Broder, and Birgitte's mom. You can't simply accept such a generous offer like that right away. But Gunnvald was crystal clear: it would be great to have people staying in his house. Besides, he said, he thought Astrid could do with some relief, since she had to put up with such an ancient best friend for the rest of the year.

If Astrid hadn't already been sure that Gunnvald was the best best friend in the whole world, she was sure of it now.

"What would I do without you, Gunnvald?" she said, smiling, as he put her back down.

The rest of the vacation was as fantastic as only a winter break in Glimmerdal can be. It goes without saying: new friends, sledding, bonfires, big dinners, shouting, yelling, and fiddle music.

But there was one person who couldn't be merry all the time, and that was Gunnvald. Each night, after everybody else had gone to bed, he sat in his kitchen with the letter in his hands, thinking. And each night, he started writing a reply. A reply that he threw in the trash every morning, running his hand roughly through his hair.

"Heidi . . ." he whispered on one of those mornings.

That little name trembled in the air. Nobody in Glimmerdal had spoken it for almost thirty years.

HEIDI

There's a secret place in Glimmerdal. You have to follow the river upstream from Gunnvald's farm all the way to Glimmerdal Shieling, the mountain pasture where the animals graze in summer, and then even farther up. But it's impossible to find the secret place if you don't know where it is. And nobody in Glimmerdal knows. Not even Astrid. Nobody's been to that place for almost thirty years.

And in a city far away from Glimmerdal, somebody has been longing to return to that secret place every day for all those years.

CHAPTER ELEVEN

In which Gunnvald and Astrid move Gladiator to the summer barn, and there is an accident with a coffeepot

I t was almost March. The snow was melting on the south-facing slopes. The vacationers had left and promised to come back at Easter. The sun was shining for longer every day, and there was a hint of spring in the air that made your legs tingle. But not everybody felt like that. For Gunnvald, it was as if the gloom of winter had stuck and wouldn't let go.

Quite often when Astrid came over, he would just be sitting there, staring out the window.

"What are you thinking about?" Astrid would ask him.

"Humph" was all Gunnvald would say.

One day, when she came barging through the door

without knocking, some photographs were laid out on the kitchen table. As soon as Astrid appeared, Gunnvald swept them all up.

"What were those photos of?" she asked.

"Humph," said Gunnvald.

Another day, Gunnvald was sitting there reading a green book. He slammed it shut when Astrid came in and hid it under the table.

"What book's that?" Astrid asked.

"Humph," said Gunnvald.

"I think Gunnvald's going senile, Dad," Astrid told her father later. Her voice was sad. It's not much fun if your best friend is going senile.

"Hmm," said her dad.

Astrid stamped her foot, giving Snorri the hiccups. "Can't people stop saying 'humph' and 'hmm' in this place?"

She might as well try to cheer up that old fool, Astrid thought as she stood in the farmyard one day.

She'd dug out her bike for the first time that year. Snorri was hovering above her, making a racket. Back when they were teaching Snorri to fly, they used to sit him on Astrid's bike helmet. He would stay on her helmet until she'd gotten up enough speed that he could let go. Then he'd fly. But once you've taught a seagull to do something, that's it. Snorri still came screeching every time Astrid took out her bike, even though he was no longer a little chick.

"You're as heavy as a pregnant goose, Snorri," Astrid grumbled. "Fly on your own!"

But Snorri grabbed on to her helmet, although he looked quite ruffled.

Gunnvald watched Astrid and Snorri's pyramid on wheels as they rode up across his farmyard.

"Snorri's brooding," Astrid explained. "Sitting up there, he keeps my brain warm and makes ideas hatch straight out of my head."

"Humph," Gunnvald said grumpily. "Then maybe you and that rowdy seagull can hatch an idea about how I'm going to move Gladiator up to the summer barn without getting killed in the process. Eh?"

Astrid scratched her cheek for a moment. "That depends," she mumbled, lifting Snorri down.

Gladiator is Gunnvald's ram. He'd bought him in Barkvika the year before, and he'd been nothing but trouble ever since.

"That ram's the worst deal I've ever made in my entire sorry life," Gunnvald had said the first time they tried to get Gladiator into the barn. Astrid remembered that her dad and aunts had come over to lend a hand too.

Now Gladiator had to be moved back out of the main barn. It would be lambing season soon, so more space was needed inside. Astrid asked Gunnvald whether they should just get her dad, like they'd done when Gladiator had to go inside. Surely they could coax him out again if they did it as a team, she thought.

"Nah," Gunnvald grunted. "Creeping cranberries, I should jolly well be able to move my own ram. I just need some more coffee first." He went inside.

Astrid sat there, peering up at the field where the summer barn was. Imagine the ram having a whole little barn to himself instead of having to listen to the gossiping of a mob of pregnant ewes. Any reasonable ram would volunteer to go up there.

"Can it really be that hard?" she muttered to herself.

*　*　*

Gunnvald's barn is a merry mess, with junk and hay all piled on top of each other. But the sheep like it. Astrid said hello to some of them, then she scooped some sheep nuts into the bottom of a bucket and walked over to Gladiator's pen. His eyes were bright green in the semidarkness. He had an enormous head. It grew even larger as he came closer to find out who Astrid was.

"Squaaawk!" Snorri screeched behind her.

"Shut your beak! You'll only annoy him!" Astrid's voice was stern. She turned back toward Gladiator. "Listen here, you beast: the sun's shining outside, and just behind the farmhouse there's a fantastic vacation palace for you. Come on, now."

She opened the pen with trembling hands, slowly stepping backward while shaking the bucket. Gladiator heard the wonderful sound of treats and followed her at a steady pace. Astrid pushed the barn door open with her backside and reversed out into the spring air. Poor Gladiator: he hadn't seen the sun for many months. Blinded, he stood in the doorway, squinting. Astrid had to shake the feed bucket even harder so he could follow the sound.

She felt quite pleased with herself as she opened the gate to the field. Gladiator was still following her as obediently as a lamb.

"I sure have a way with animals," Astrid boasted to Snorri, who was sitting on a gatepost, watching closely.

But then things stopped going according to plan. No sooner had Astrid opened the gate than Gladiator shoved her from the side, almost knocking her over. That maniac had gotten his eyesight back!

"Uh-oh," Astrid whispered, starting to walk faster.

The ram kept on nudging her, and eventually Astrid realized that she'd have to run away if she wanted to avoid being butted hard. Her lion curls danced in the spring sunshine as she legged it toward the summer barn, Gladiator following in hot pursuit.

"The bucket!" Astrid sighed.

What a fool she was. It was no wonder he was chasing her. With a mighty fling, she threw the bucket as far as she could, sending sheep nuts scattering across the field. But Gladiator didn't give a lemming's tail about that now: all he wanted was to catch Astrid. Maybe he was like a bull and just ran after anything red?

"Your hair's as red as a barn door at sunset," Astrid's granny had once told her. At the time, Astrid had been sure that nothing lovelier had ever been said to anybody on the planet since records began. But right now she wished she had black or blond or brown hair. She would even have made do with gray hair at that moment.

Then she fell. There was a wretched rock there, all ready to trip her. She just managed to throw herself to one side as the wild ram thundered toward her. He grazed her elbow with his rock-hard head.

"Ow!"

Ugh, it was so typical of Gunnvald to buy such a terrible ram! And just think: this ram would be the father of half of Gunnvald's lambs. He was going to end up with the world's loopiest sheep.

Now Gladiator would be coming back for her, sure as mutton.

Astrid clambered to her feet and stumbled on. She'd had an idea—she could seek safety on the roof of the

117

summer barn. There are many things rams can do, but they can't climb. Astrid, on the other hand, is more closely related to the apes than most people, as Auntie Idun says. She took a quick turn to the right, just as Gladiator threw himself at her again, then five steps over to the barn, where she jumped up onto the pallet leaning against the wall like a ladder, and then grabbed the roof with her hands. Astrid dangled there for a while, thrashing about between heaven and earth. Gladiator managed to butt her on the leg, but eventually she succeeded in swinging one foot onto the roof and was able to twist the rest of her body up after it.

She was safe.

Snorri flew up and landed next to her. Down in the field, the furious Gladiator stamped his hoof hard and insistently on the ground, again and again. Astrid pulled herself farther away from the edge of the roof. Then she took a deep breath and shouted out into the spring air of Glimmerdal:

"Gunnvaaaaaald!"

*　*　*

118

"What in every blasted Saturday's burnt gruel and porridge are you doing up there?"

Gunnvald squinted against the sun, clearly annoyed. Astrid pointed down at the ram. She could see Gunnvald sigh. He shouted to her that now she'd gotten herself into such a hopeless fix, she could just stay up there. Gladiator would probably be fed up with waiting after a while and go into his nice summer barn. Then Astrid could climb down and slam the door shut.

"No!" she shouted. "What if he never gets fed up? You have to come over here and distract him."

"Do I look like I've got red hair to distract him with?" Gunnvald plonked his coffeepot down on the steps outside his house and went inside.

"Gunnvald!"

Was he just going to leave her sitting there? She knew Gunnvald was a stubborn old mule, and he'd been worse than ever recently, but Astrid would never have expected this. Imagine leaving your best friend on a roof to fend for herself with a deadly ram from Barkvika below her!

Astrid had just decided never to visit Gunnvald ever

again for the rest of her life, when he came back out with his Christmas tablecloth. She would've recognized that tablecloth from the other side of the glen, as she was the one who'd embroidered it. With her own hands. The whole tablecloth was covered with bullfinches and Christmas trees made out of tiny little cross-stitches.

"Do you have to make it so big, Astrid?" her teacher, Dagny, had asked her when Astrid was still toiling away at the enormous tablecloth—which was supposed to be for Christmas, after all—long into February.

"Yes, because Gunnvald's a big man with a big table," Astrid had answered.

And Gunnvald had been just as pleased with the tablecloth as Astrid had hoped. He'd almost cried a little tear when he opened the parcel.

"Holy muskrat," Astrid whispered now, when she realized what Gunnvald was about to do.

He walked into the field with the tablecloth flapping about in one hand. Then he stood up straight like a general.

"*Olé!*" said Gunnvald, stomping on the ground.

Suddenly Gladiator wasn't the slightest bit interested in Astrid on the roof anymore.

There was a bullfight in Glimmerdal that day. True enough, no weapons were used, and true enough, it was between an old and stiff bullfighter and a crazed ram from Barkvika instead of a bull, but still. Gunnvald swung the tablecloth so elegantly that you would've thought he'd been bullfighting all his life. Time after time, Gladiator thundered down the field, ramming his head straight through the cross-stitched bullfinches and out into thin air. The old matador glanced up at Astrid triumphantly and took a bow. *Swoosh,* there went Gladiator diving into the tablecloth again. It looked pretty impressive.

But gradually Gunnvald found himself on the back foot. He started waving the tablecloth more frantically, and Gladiator got closer to hitting him each time. Eventually Gunnvald was running around the field with the tablecloth flying out like a red flag behind him.

"*Olé!*" he howled in desperation.

"Get up here, Gunnvald!" Astrid waved at him, but Gunnvald just shook his fist.

"Blasted blackberries, I'm going to get that psychopath of a ram into the summer barn if it's the last thing I do!" he bellowed, rushing toward the open door.

Then the enormous Gunnvald ran inside the summer barn with a crash, closely followed by a galloping Gladiator. Snorri took off from the roof like a jet aircraft.

After a few seconds of tremendous racket, the door slammed shut. Astrid crawled forward nervously and peeked down.

"Are you alive, Gunnvald?" she asked warily.

Gunnvald dried the sweat from his forehead with the tablecloth. "That's the last time I buy anything in Barkvika," he said, getting into position so Astrid could reach his shoulders with her feet and climb down.

It's hard to believe what happened next. There was Gunnvald, who'd just put on a breakneck performance of a bullfight and come away from it without a scratch, and then he went and tripped over his own coffeepot. Astrid was walking just behind him and saw as Gunnvald, who'd forgotten that he'd put his coffeepot on the steps, caught his foot on the handle, lost his balance, and fell as far down the stone steps as he was tall.

There was a terrible sound of bones breaking.

And then silence.

CHAPTER TWELVE

In which Gunnvald is
mightily scared in the hospital

It was such a lovely day in Glimmerdal. People had opened their windows for the first time since the winter. The mountains were gleaming, and you could almost see the snow melting on the slopes. It's strange that such terrible things can happen on days like that.

But they can. Right at the top of Glimmerdal, an old man was lying by the steps outside his house, and next to that man was his little best friend, sitting there and looking anxiously down the glen.

"If you die, Gunnvald, I'll kill you," Astrid said. She had a lump in her throat, but she wasn't crying, because then Gunnvald would be even more scared. Poor, poor Gunnvald.

Astrid had done everything Dagny, her teacher, had taught her to do if there was an accident. She'd called for an ambulance, and she'd draped a woolen blanket over Gunnvald. Luckily he hadn't fainted. He's so enormous that she would've needed a winch to put him in the recovery position.

"It's nothing serious," she said to comfort him, but she didn't believe her own words.

It looked serious. Gunnvald's face had gone gray, and he wasn't saying anything.

But when the ambulance finally arrived, Gunnvald suddenly regained his speech, and with a vengeance. He turned into as much of a beast as Gladiator, yelling at the ambulance workers for all he was worth. There was no way he was going to any hospital! He'd sooner lie there and die in the peace of the steps outside his home.

The poor paramedics.

"You can't lie here and die," Astrid said in a strict voice. "I'll come with you."

Then Gunnvald closed his mouth and squeezed her hand so hard it made her whimper.

"Shouldn't you be getting home, little one?" the ambulance man asked as he prepared the stretcher.

Astrid shook her head. The paramedics looked at Gunnvald's hand clutching Astrid's. They would've needed pneumatic pliers to loosen that grip.

"Then you'd better come with us."

But when Astrid and Gunnvald were in the ambulance, Gunnvald let go of her hand all by himself.

"Astrid," he struggled to say. "I need to take the letter. The letter. It's on the bookshelf."

Astrid didn't ask him which letter he meant. Even though she'd neither seen nor heard about it since earlier that winter, she realized which one it must be. The letter saying that Anna Zimmermann had died. She ran inside and wasn't surprised in the slightest when she found it on the bookshelf. But she was a little surprised when she saw how frayed the envelope was. Gunnvald must have read the letter hundreds of times. Astrid grabbed it and ran outside.

Then they set off. They drove all the way to town, to the big hospital.

* * *

It was a tough day. Gunnvald was sure that he was going to die. The doctors and the nurses were busy, almost only speaking among themselves. Astrid had never been ignored that much in her life. Eventually she grabbed a doctor by his coat so he had to stop and talk to her whether he wanted to or not.

"Is Gunnvald going to die?" she asked sharply.

The doctor looked at her, astonished. "No, of course not."

"Do you promise?"

The doctor promised. So that she was sure, he took Astrid by the hand and gave her a good old-fashioned word-of-honor pledge.

Gunnvald wasn't going to die, but try explaining that to a stubborn old mule who has never been admitted to a hospital before. He was beside himself with worry. Astrid comforted him, talking to him and holding his hand, but now and then she couldn't help getting angry.

"If you don't calm down, I'm going to take you for recycling!" she shouted at one point. "Then they can turn you from the fool you're being today into a new, nicer Gunnvald!"

When Astrid's dad appeared at the door, she was completely worn out, and flung herself into his arms. Astrid's poor dad had thought it was Astrid who had been injured. When he'd come home from the shop, Sally had been out by the road, waving him down. Spluttering, she'd managed to tell him that she'd seen Astrid up on the roof of Gunnvald's summer barn, and that the ambulance had gone past soon afterward.

"Poor girl," Sally had wailed, putting her hand over her heart. "She may have been injured for life!"

Now Astrid's dad held her close; he was so relieved that it was Gunnvald and not her in the hospital bed. "You've done a really good job, Astrid," he said.

Everybody was suddenly less busy. The doctors explained what had happened and answered the questions Astrid's dad asked from behind his beard. Gunnvald had a nasty fracture to the neck of his femur—his thigh bone—they said, and he'd need an operation that very evening. He'd also broken his ankle, but they wouldn't be able to operate on that for a few days. The swelling had to go down first.

"I want to go home." Gunnvald sniffed. He was calmer now. They'd pumped a boatload of medicine into him. But he couldn't go home. It would be many weeks before Gunnvald could return to Glimmerdal. First he needed an operation on his thigh, and then he needed an operation on his ankle, and after that he'd have to get fit enough to walk again.

"I'm going to die," said Gunnvald.

"Me too," Astrid muttered glumly. "I'm going to be bored to death."

CHAPTER THIRTEEN

In which Astrid reads the green book, and Gunnvald gives her a secret mission

There would be twice as much for Astrid and her dad to do now. Lambing would be starting in a couple of weeks, and they'd have to look after both their own sheep and Gunnvald's. Luckily, there were lots of good helpers in Glimmerdal. Peter had volunteered to lend a hand with the lambing. It would all be fine, Astrid reassured Gunnvald over the phone. But Gunnvald didn't think so. He still thought he was going to die.

"Stop being silly," said Astrid, promising to feed Hulda.

The next day, when Astrid got off the school bus down at the roadside by the boxes where their mail was delivered, she trudged up the hill to Gunnvald's farm instead of her own. She prepared the cat's food and sat down in the rocking chair, watching Hulda tuck in. The clock ticked. Astrid rocked back and forth. It was strange being there without Gunnvald. She looked around the empty kitchen, her gaze landing on the bookshelf. There, at one end of the third shelf, was where she'd found the letter the day before.

Astrid stood up. Wasn't that the green book? The one that Gunnvald had been reading once when she'd come barging in; the one he'd slammed shut and hidden under the table? Astrid tilted her head. *Heidi,* it said on the spine. She pulled it out. It looked like a book for grown-ups, as there wasn't a picture on the front cover. Or maybe it had just been torn off. But when Astrid opened the book, she saw a beautiful illustration of a boy with a hat, a girl with curly dark hair, and some goats.

Astrid took the book and sat back down in the rocking chair. The pages smelled old. To begin with, there were lots of difficult names, some talk about a mother's grandmother who was somebody else's cousin, and other

131

things that Astrid didn't understand, so she was about to put the book back down again, but then it became more interesting.

It was about a little girl called Heidi. She was only five at the start, and both her parents were dead. Now she was on her way up the mountains with her aunt, who was called Aunt Deta.

"Aunt Deta." Astrid tried saying the name out loud. She liked it. But she didn't like the aunt. She wasn't very kind.

Heidi, the girl with the curly dark hair, was going to her grandfather's house, Aunt Deta had decided. Heidi's grandfather lived far up in the mountains, all alone with two goats. All the villagers were afraid of him because he was angry and dangerous and had eyebrows that had grown to meet each other in the middle. When they heard that Aunt Deta was going to leave Heidi with him, the villagers tried everything they could think of to persuade her to change her mind. How could she leave an innocent young girl up there with that terrible man? Some people even said that her grandfather had once murdered another man in a fight. Still, Aunt Deta took the orphaned Heidi up the steep mountain slopes. She couldn't look after her anymore, she said, even though she'd promised Heidi's mother that she would. She didn't have the time. Heidi would have to stay with her grandfather, no matter what the villagers thought.

What would happen to Heidi all alone up there with her terrible grandfather? Astrid read on, her heart in her mouth. Luckily, as the book went on, she grew sure the villagers had been wrong. Heidi's grandfather didn't seem that bad even though he was a bit grumpy. He lived in a small cabin up where the wind blew through the spruce trees and the mountains gleamed.

It must be like the mountain pasture at Glimmerdal Shieling, Astrid thought. She remembered how the wind whistled around the walls when they spent the night in the old hut up there in the summer. Lots of beautiful flowers grew there in the summer months too, just like in the book about Heidi.

Astrid forgot she was sitting in Gunnvald's kitchen. She lost track of time; she lost track of everything. It was almost as if she had become Heidi, as if the whole story were taking place in Glimmerdal. Heidi slept in the hayloft at her grandfather's house; Astrid had often slept in the hay too, in the summer. And the best part was when Heidi got to go with Peter the goatherd, herding goats far, far up into the mountains, where the sunset lit the snow on fire in the evenings. Just like up on Storr Peak, Astrid thought. She could picture it quite clearly.

Heidi was happier living with her grandfather than she'd ever been before. She looked after the two goats, Schwänli and Bärli, and she drank goat's milk, which made her strong. And her fierce grandfather was nothing but kind to her.

"Astrid?"

It was Astrid's dad. He came into Gunnvald's kitchen carrying a bag. "We'd better get a toothbrush and some clean undies for our patient in town," he said. "What are you reading?"

Astrid held up the green book, and her dad squinted to read the title. *"Heidi."* His face took on a strange expression. "Where did you find that?"

Astrid pointed at the bookshelf.

"Hmm," said her dad.

Astrid didn't tell Gunnvald she'd found the green book.

Somehow she felt that he wouldn't like it. His mood was still as tangled as an inside-out sweater. Everything was wrong at the hospital: the doctors ran around like whipped cats, the nurses weren't doing things properly, and the food tasted like canned crow.

"On top of all that, I'm fresh out of snus," Gunnvald moaned.

When Astrid's dad went down to the shop to buy the poor man some more of that disgusting snus, Gunnvald immediately stopped complaining and beckoned to Astrid. He looked over at the door to make sure nobody was listening.

"I've got an important mission for you, Astrid."

The curtains fluttered a little, the rays of sunshine making a beautiful pattern on the floor.

"Do you want me to blow up the coffeepot into a thousand pieces?" Astrid asked.

She was very welcome to do that, Gunnvald said, but that wasn't the mission. He glanced over at the door yet again, then he put his hand under his shirt collar and pulled out a letter.

"You've got to mail this."

Astrid took the letter in astonishment.

"This is important," Gunnvald went on. "If I die—"

"Stop going on about all this dying," Astrid scolded him. "You're not going to die."

"You never know. Operations are dangerous," Gunnvald said, clearly scared. "I only just survived that thigh bone operation. Now I've got to have an operation on my ankle in three days. This might be the last time you see me."

Astrid huffed. Then she bowed her head to look at the address. She couldn't believe her eyes. *Ms. A. Zimmermann.*

"Anna Zimmermann!" she shouted.

Gunnvald's finger shot up to his lips, and he said "Shh!" so loudly that he almost blew himself out of bed. "It's a secret, you little troll!"

"All right, but Gunnvald, you can't send letters to dead people! Are you losing it?"

Gunnvald reassured Astrid that he wasn't losing anything. "The address doesn't say 'Ms. A. Zimmermann, c/o Heaven, ZZ99 2AZ,' does it? No, it's a perfectly normal address: a beautiful long address in Germany."

"Fine, but you said that Anna Zimmermann was dead." Astrid didn't understand. "Isn't she dead?"

"Stop going on about all this dying," Gunnvald barked. He didn't want to explain. He just took her hand. "Dearest Astrid, this is an old man's last wish."

"What would you do without me?" Astrid said, putting the letter in her jacket pocket without waiting for an answer.

Three days later, the same evening that Gunnvald had his operation—and, to his great surprise, survived it splendidly—a mailman in Germany put an envelope through a letter slot in a grand old city building. The person inside the house slowly picked it up. Then the letter was read many, many times over, and the person who'd read it stared out the big windows, deep in thought.

CHAPTER FOURTEEN

In which a mysterious woman and a terrifying dog turn up in Glimmerdal

On a soggy spring day one week after the operation on Gunnvald's ankle, a tall woman with an orange backpack and an enormous dog walked off the ferry at the wharf. She stood there for a moment, completely still. When her nose caught the spring breeze blowing down the glen, she closed her eyes and tightened her grip on the dog's leash. Her face softened a little, but only for a second. Then it hardened again. The dog growled at the sparrows underneath the old ice-cream table, which hardly improved matters.

The woman started walking up the narrow road, slush

splashing around her feet. She walked past the closed-down snack bar, the shop, and the hair salon. Theo was standing at the door to the salon, but he didn't ask her whether she wanted a haircut. Theo had never, ever seen so much tousled hair on one woman before. He was speechless. Standing between his legs was his little poodle, Matisse, who looked at the giant canine monster and squeaked in terror.

Behind the curtains of the few houses up the glen, people whispered to one another as the tall lady went past. Nobody had seen her before. She was probably heading to Hagen's Wellness Retreat, they thought. But she had a dog. Dogs were strictly forbidden at the camp, like most other things. She'd probably have to turn back when she got there and take the afternoon boat home.

"What a giant lady!"

"Have you ever seen hair like that?"

"And look at that dog! I wouldn't like to meet those two in a dark alley."

People kept whispering away behind their curtains, while the woman and her dog continued up past Peter and his mother's house. Eventually they came to Hagen's

Wellness Retreat. Surely that must be where they were going? No. The woman and the dog went right on by. They didn't so much as glance at Hagen's Wellness Retreat. Slowly and unshakably, they walked on up the glen, through the enchanted forest and past Sally's house.

Now not a soul in the world could see them or where they were going anymore. Astrid's dad had taken Sally to the drugstore in Barkvika that day. Gunnvald was in the hospital. And Astrid? Sitting in Gunnvald's kitchen, reading the green book about Heidi, Astrid barely knew she was in Glimmerdal at all.

She could hardly breathe, as now Heidi's idiotic aunt had suddenly decided to go and get her, just when Heidi had grown so fond of her grandfather, and he of her. Aunt Deta, that old bag, just came and snatched Heidi. Her grandfather was furious.

"Take her and ruin her, but do not bring her before my sight again," he shouted at Aunt Deta as she dragged little Heidi down from the mountain. Poor Heidi, and her poor grandfather! Astrid was so angry with Aunt Deta that her insides boiled.

Heidi had to travel to a city called Frankfurt, where she was going to work for a terribly rich family as a playmate for a girl who was sickly and in a wheelchair.

"Frankfurt," Astrid muttered to herself. Where had she heard of Frankfurt before? She kept reading for a while. Then she suddenly remembered: it was in the address on the letter that Gunnvald had written! It had been sent to Frankfurt. Astrid frowned and patted the green book. Why exactly did Gunnvald have that book?

Clara, the rich girl in the wheelchair, was very nice. She thought Heidi was the best thing that had ever happened to her, as she brought the old house in Frankfurt to life. Heidi had come straight from the mountains, where she'd slept in the hay and played with goats, and she didn't know how to behave in such a fancy house. So she made lots of mistakes and did strange things that seemed funny to Clara and the servants. Astrid laughed too at all the things Heidi got up to, but the book's strict Miss Rottenmeier was in no laughing mood. She was so horrible that it sent a shiver down Astrid's spine. Miss Rottenmeier thought it was scandalous that Heidi had been let into the house. And poor Heidi missed her grandfather and her mountains so much that she could hardly bring herself to eat. She didn't dare tell anybody either, since she was so scared that Clara would get upset and even more sickly if she told her that she didn't want to stay there and play with her.

One day, Heidi couldn't take it any longer. She had to see her mountains! If she could climb to the top of the high church tower, then maybe she'd catch a glimpse of them. Heidi slipped out into the town without permission, and a boy helped her find the tower. At the top, the tower keeper lifted her up so she could look out across Frankfurt, and then Heidi was so disappointed that it almost made Astrid cry as she sat there reading about it in Gunnvald's empty kitchen. Heidi still couldn't see her mountains. There were just buildings, buildings, and more buildings as far as the eye could see. Were there really cities that big? Imagine how lonely and helpless Heidi must have felt!

Suddenly there was somebody opening the door latch outside, and Astrid heard steps in the hallway. It had to be her dad returning from Barkvika. He was a bit early, really, she thought; she wished she could have finished the book first.

"Dad, Heidi's—" said Astrid, just as the kitchen door opened.

She didn't get any further.

It wasn't her dad at the door.

CHAPTER FIFTEEN

In which Astrid has a scary experience and is quite stunned

Astrid is really quite brave. There aren't many things she's afraid of. She's not scared of ghosts, as she doesn't believe in them. She's not scared of being alone, because she's so used to it. She's not scared of heights, of the dark, of strangers, of speed, of water, of fire, of spiders, of mice, or of thunder. And she's not scared of Mr. Hagen either. But there's one thing Astrid is scared of, and she's so scared of it that it makes up for everything else. Astrid Glimmerdal is so abso-heart-stopping-lutely scared of dogs that you wouldn't believe it.

The only dog Astrid dares to stroke is teeny-tiny Matisse at Theo's hair salon. But she does it as seldom as she can, and usually makes considerable detours to avoid going anywhere near a dog.

So the fact that there was suddenly a lady in Gunnvald's kitchen who was a total stranger to Astrid was one thing. And the fact that this stranger was the tallest woman Astrid had ever seen was another thing. But Astrid would've taken all this in stride if it hadn't been for the dog, because suddenly, with no warning at all, there was a black-haired beast with a flat snout and a shiny coat standing in Gunnvald's kitchen. And it was growling. Poor Hulda arched her back and dived under the sofa like a misfired rocket. Astrid was so frightened that she couldn't even say "help."

"Who are you?" the lady asked.

What on earth? What kind of a question was that?

"Uh . . ." Astrid stuttered, stiffening and squeezing herself up on top of the chair.

The lady pulled the dog's leash and stomped out. Astrid could hear her rummaging around in the farmyard. Shaking, she got up from the chair, and the book about Heidi fell to the floor with a smack.

When the woman came thundering back in, Astrid was still as white as a sheet beneath her spring freckles.

"I've tied the dog to the flagpole. Don't go near him. He bites," the lady said in a gravelly voice. Then she didn't say any more. The door was open. She probably thought Astrid should go. This was so wrong!

"Who are you?" Astrid asked, trying to sound stern, but she was far too curious. The lady was quite stunning, even though she was scruffily dressed. Her skin was tanned, and her eyes were so dark they seemed black. Astrid thought she looked like an enormous version of a girl in a film she'd once seen called *Ronja, Robbersdaughter.*

The lady didn't answer. Her eyes scanned the room, lingering on Gunnvald's fiddle and then on the book on the floor. She still didn't say a word. Then she looked at Astrid, sizing her up.

"You don't live here, do you?"

Astrid shook her head. "It's Gunnvald's house, but he's in the hospital. I live on the other side of the glen."

"Yes, I should've realized, with red hair like yours."

Astrid's jaw dropped. The lady sat down on Astrid's usual

146

chair as if it were the most natural thing in the world to sit right there. On Astrid's chair.

"Are you Sigurd's sister?"

Astrid was even more stunned. "No, he's my dad."

The lady, who had been looking out the window, turned to Astrid with a surprised expression. "Well, I never," she murmured.

As usual, the little thunderbolt of Glimmerdal showed that she was more courteous and welcoming than the average person.

"Would you like a cup of coffee?" she asked, thinking that it couldn't do any harm to use the pot one more time before blowing it up.

The lady didn't want any coffee.

"What exactly are you doing here?" she asked instead.

"What am I doing here?" Astrid said, confused. "I'm feeding Hulda."

"Do you know Gunnvald, then?" the lady asked harshly.

Astrid told her that Gunnvald was her neighbor, godfather, and best friend.

"Is that so?" The lady sniffed, sizing up Astrid yet again.

Most vacationers in Glimmerdal look at Astrid like that when they first meet her: from her lion's mane of curls on top, past her freckled face, over her clothes, which are always a little messy, down to her feet, where Astrid has one foot that points forward and one that points a little out to the side. But Astrid had never been scrutinized as thoroughly as this before. She almost felt she should have a little glance at herself, to make sure she didn't look weird or anything.

"I think you should go home," the lady said. "I'll feed the cat from now on."

"No way!" Astrid crossed her arms decisively, but the lady just smirked at her.

"You'll do as I say," she said quite simply, nodding in the direction of the flagpole.

Astrid gulped and fished her hat down from the hook where it was hanging. "I'll be back," she said in the calmest voice she could manage.

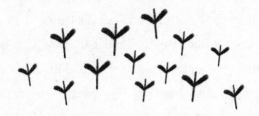

CHAPTER SIXTEEN

In which Dad reveals
something really shocking

Sometimes it's extremely annoying being a child. Astrid had never noticed it much before now, though. Most people in Glimmerdal treated her like an adult. She got to help make decisions, and people didn't have any secrets that she didn't know about. At least that's what Astrid thought.

That day, everything was turned upside down. Astrid suddenly found out something that everybody else had known all her life but nobody had told her. Astrid's best friend, her dad, her mom, her granny, her grandpa, and everybody else had a secret. Even Sally had known: she can't keep so much as a little fart of a secret, yet she had never told Astrid this hugely important thing.

And this is how Astrid found out the truth:

Once she'd walked calmly out of Gunnvald's kitchen and continued in an enormous arc around the flagpole, Astrid Glimmerdal started running like she'd never run before. She reached the bridge just as her dad was turning off to drop Sally at her house.

"Dad, there's a woman making herself all at home at Gunnvald's place! And a dog and . . ."

Astrid's dad helped Sally out of the car.

"What are you saying?" Sally asked, all flustered, squeezing Astrid's dad's elbow so hard that the pain made him open his mouth wide.

Astrid told them breathlessly about the tall woman with the tousled hair and the black eyes, while her dad took Sally and her bags up the steps to her house.

"Dad, she knew who you were!" Astrid shouted.

"Did she?" he said, surprised, looking up the track to Gunnvald's farm.

He stroked his beard pensively, then suddenly stopped. For the first time in her life, Astrid saw her dad lose his usual calm for a brief moment.

"It can't be Heidi, can it?" he asked Sally.

"Heidi?" Sally echoed in disbelief.

Astrid stood there like a big question mark, while Sally rummaged frantically in her shopping bag for her new bottle of pills.

"Heidi?" she babbled. "Heidi? After all these years? Praise the Lord!"

"Heidi?" Astrid asked, confused. "Like in the book?"

Suddenly Astrid's dad seemed in more of a hurry than Astrid could remember ever seeing him in before. She had to jog to keep up with him as they climbed the hill to Gunnvald's farm.

"Dad!"

In the farmyard, Astrid slowed down a little as her dad walked on ahead. She had to keep her distance from that horrible dog still snarling there.

When she finally reached the steps, her dad had already knocked, and the enormous woman had opened the door. They stood there for a long while, looking at each other without saying a word. Then Astrid's dad cleared his throat.

"Haven't you grown?" he said.

The lady forgot herself and a smile flickered across her face, but it quickly disappeared.

"Dad?" Astrid said from behind him. She couldn't understand what was going on.

He took her by the shoulders and placed her in front of him. "I understand you've already met each other. This is Astrid, my daughter," he said proudly. Then he nodded toward the lady at the door. "And Astrid, this is Heidi." He squeezed the back of her neck a little before he added, "Gunnvald's daughter."

No way! Astrid stared first at her dad, then at the woman in the doorway, and then back at her dad. The dog snarled behind them.

"Gunnvald doesn't have a daughter." Astrid's voice was quite certain, even though she now realized that this Heidi did actually look like a chip off the old block, almost as if she'd been blown straight out of Gunnvald's enormous nose.

"He doesn't have a daughter!" she repeated.

The lady gave Astrid a cold look. "No, I guess he doesn't," she snapped. Then she nodded to Astrid's dad.

"Good to see you're still hanging on, Sigurd, but I can manage on my own."

She closed the door.

It wasn't an easy trip for Astrid's dad as he walked back down the hill from Gunnvald's farm with Astrid, fetched the car, and drove them up to their farm. Astrid was getting very angry. What kind of trickery was all this?

"Gunnvald had a German girlfriend for a few months when he was young," Astrid's dad began warily. "A girl he met at some fiddle music thing or other in Germany."

"Anna Zimmermann?" Astrid asked.

Her dad looked at her in surprise. "Yes, Anna Zimmermann. But it didn't last very long, from what I've heard. Anna disappeared and then four years later she turned up in Glimmerdal. She had a four-year-old girl with her, called Heidi."

Astrid stared at him openmouthed.

"Gunnvald had no idea he was a dad until the day he saw the girl on his doorstep. Anna Zimmermann stayed for a few days in Glimmerdal. Then she left, leaving the child with Gunnvald." Astrid's dad scratched his beard and shook his head. "It certainly caused a bit of a commotion. Nobody could see how it would work. All his life, Gunnvald had never had anybody other than himself to think of, then suddenly he had a four-year-old to look after."

"But, but . . . ?" Astrid stuttered.

"Anna Zimmermann was a famous violinist," her dad explained. "She traveled all over the world performing concerts. She must have thought it would be better for Heidi to live with Gunnvald."

"Heidi lived in Glimmerdal? With Gunnvald?"

Astrid was completely stunned. Her dad nodded.

"Yes, she grew up here. We used to play together every single day when we were little. We were always running around in the mountains, and Heidi taught me and my little brothers all sorts of things."

It was unusual for Astrid's dad to say so much all at once. It was as if somebody had opened a secret door inside him, and now the words poured out.

"Anna came to visit every now and then. She was a very elegant lady. She called Heidi 'Adelheid,' because apparently that was her real name, and she brought lots of expensive clothes for her and spoke German to her. My brothers and I used to get fancy foreign chocolate. One time, Anna brought Heidi a miniature fiddle, and then the next time she brought her a slightly bigger one. But she was never here for very long. And when Anna left, Heidi would put away her fancy clothes and put on her scruffy old ones. But she played the fiddles. They used to play together, her and Gunnvald. She took lessons in town and got pretty good after a while."

"But," Astrid said again. She couldn't understand why Gunnvald had never mentioned a thing about this!

"And then, when Heidi was twelve, Anna came and took her away."

"Huh?"

Astrid's dad nodded. "That was almost thirty years ago, and nobody in Glimmerdal has seen Heidi since then. The rumor was that she became as good at the violin as her mother back in Germany. I don't know whether it's true."

Astrid sat there, her arms down by her sides. She had neither strength nor energy to move.

"What did Gunnvald say, though?" she asked eventually.

Her dad's face took on a strange expression. "Gunnvald said nothing. He tore down all his pictures of Heidi and made a big bonfire in the garden with all her fancy clothes and . . ." He stopped.

"Go on," Astrid ordered him with tears in her eyes.

"I was only ten, Astrid. I can't remember very much about it," he mumbled. "But I spent a long time angry with Gunnvald about that bonfire."

They arrived at their farm and got out of the car. Snorri came screeching over, landing happily on Astrid's dad's shoulder. In the barn the ewes were bleating; they'd soon be ready for lambing. Nothing was different, and yet everything had changed.

"Why did nobody tell me?"

Astrid was very upset. There she'd gone, being best friends with a stubborn old mule, telling him all sorts of secrets like best friends should, while that numbskull hadn't said a word about having a towering daughter. Nobody had said anything!

Her dad scratched the back of his neck and glanced over at her. "Nobody's spoken about Heidi since then, Astrid. Gunnvald wouldn't be able to take it."

"What do you mean, he wouldn't be able to take it?"

Then Astrid's dad told her that one of his little brothers had once asked if Heidi was ever coming back. Gunnvald flew into such a rage that he threw a kitchen chair at the wall and said he never wanted to hear that name again for the rest of his life.

Shaking, Astrid took a deep breath. Gunnvald was the man she'd spent every single day of her life with, and she was so fond of him that the very thought made her heart creak and groan. But suddenly it was as if she didn't know him anymore.

"Do you know what your mom said when she heard the story about Gunnvald and Heidi?" her dad asked.

Astrid shook her head.

"'Gunnvald needs somebody to love again.' That's what she said. She was the one who decided that Gunnvald should be your godfather."

"Was she?"

"Yes. Of course, Gunnvald wasn't exactly desperate to be the godfather of a stinky little baby, as he himself said, but he agreed to it in the end, after your mom used all her wit and charm."

Astrid's dad smiled. "I think you've been the best medicine Gunnvald could ever have had, Astrid. He's almost behaved like a normal person for the past few years."

Astrid didn't know what to say, what to do, or what to think. Her dad stuck a dry stalk of last year's hay in his mouth.

"Life isn't always easy for some people, Astrid. It's been extra difficult for Gunnvald and Heidi."

After that, Astrid's dad didn't say any more that evening.

CHAPTER SEVENTEEN
In which Heidi reveals her awful plan

When Astrid woke the next morning, she decided to blow up the coffeepot. She dug around in her drawer and took out the massive firecrackers Auntie Eira had secretly given her the year before. That reminded Astrid: it wasn't long before she'd be ten, which would be a milestone birthday.

"It's a milestone." That's what Astrid's granny says when people have their fiftieth, sixtieth, or seventieth birthdays.

A round-number birthday is a bit bigger than a normal birthday. And ten is as round a number as you can get. Astrid had decided to have a massive party. Maybe she could put an advertisement in the local paper and have an open-house party with everybody invited?

The night before, she'd lain awake thinking about everything her dad had told her. She'd thought about Gunnvald throwing a kitchen chair at the wall, and she'd thought about Heidi's jet-black eyes. Then she'd thought about the Heidi from the book. It was strange that there was both a real Heidi and a made-up one, Astrid thought. Before she fell asleep, she'd decided to make friends with the real Heidi.

When Astrid arrived at Gunnvald's farm that morning, Heidi was sitting on the steps outside the house, drinking coffee. Just like Gunnvald usually did. Astrid had to ride her bike in a strange loop, because of the dog, and fell over like a five-year-old with no training wheels. What a horrible mutt! He snarled and growled, and looked like he wanted to eat her.

"You've got a seagull on your head," Heidi observed once Astrid had struggled to her feet.

"I know."

Astrid carefully lifted Snorri down. She needed to have a

good look at Heidi now that she knew what was what. Just think: Heidi had grown up in Glimmerdal, like her. Maybe she knew all the good places down by the river? Maybe she knew about the eagles' nest below Cairn Peak? Maybe she'd spent the night in a sleeping bag up at Glimmerdal Shieling? Had she drunk Sally's bad squash? Maybe she'd done everything Astrid did?

"This is the third time you've been here in less than a day," said Heidi. "I don't like seagulls, and I don't like visitors."

"This isn't your farm," Astrid said calmly.

Heidi laughed harshly. "Yes, it is, actually."

"No, it's Gunnvald's farm." Astrid looked firmly at Heidi.

Then the tall woman pulled a letter out of her shirt pocket. Astrid recognized it. It was the letter she'd mailed for Gunnvald just over a week ago, the one addressed to Ms. A. Zimmermann. It suddenly dawned on her that Ms. A. Zimmermann wasn't the late Anna Zimmermann, as she'd thought: Ms. A. Zimmermann was Heidi. Astrid's dad had told her the day before that Heidi's real name was Adelheid.

The letter was frayed at the edges. Astrid was starting

to regret having sent it. She should've eaten it instead.

"Gunnvald thought he was going to kick the bucket," Heidi said quite directly. "He's given the farm to me. That's what it says in this letter, black on white. The whole place is mine now."

What on earth? Astrid frowned. But only briefly. If Heidi really was Gunnvald's daughter, then she would've inherited his farm anyway. It was hardly a scandal. Astrid shrugged and acted as if she didn't care.

Then Heidi stood up, towering over Astrid. "Do you know what I'm going to do with this farm, Astrid?"

Astrid shook her head. Was she going to live there, perhaps? Or start an organic farm, like that man over in Barkvika?

"I'm going to sell it," Heidi announced. "I'm going to sell the whole lot and never set foot here again."

"You're going to sell the farm? Now?" Astrid was so surprised, she was practically shouting.

"That's right. As soon as possible."

The little thunderbolt of Glimmerdal stared at Heidi, terror stricken. "Where's Gunnvald going to live, then?"

Heidi put the letter back in her shirt pocket and spat out some snus. "I couldn't care less about Gunnvald," she said matter-of-factly.

Then everything went black for Astrid. Never had a single sentence made her so angry. Something snapped in her head, and for the second time in her life, Astrid got into a fight. This time, though, she should have thought about it a little more carefully. It was like a squirrel attacking a dinosaur. Heidi caught her in midair and held her in an iron grip. It was as easy as pie for her.

"You're not allowed not to care about Gunnvald!" Astrid yelled fiercely, kicking and thrashing about.

"Sure I am," Heidi said calmly. "Stop screaming."

But Astrid wouldn't stop, because Gunnvald was her best friend and had treated her kindly her whole life. And if Gunnvald couldn't come home, then he'd die; she was sure of that. Then what would Astrid do? What was Glimmerdal without Gunnvald? The very thought made her feel all dark inside. It wasn't even possible.

"You can't sell it! I'll tell everybody in all of Glimmerdal, so nobody will buy it," Astrid snarled.

Heidi let go of her. "Tell as many people as you like, Astrid. I'd speak to that guy down at the vacation camp if I were you; he's practically bought the place already. He said something about building some cabins. There's a better view from up here than down there in the hollow."

That was *it*. She had to be the craziest woman Astrid had ever met. You couldn't sell Gunnvald's farm to Mr. Hagen! If you did, it would be over Astrid Glimmerdal's dead body. She had to put a stop to this, and she knew exactly where to start. One thing was for sure: if it hadn't been for the coffeepot, all this misery would've been avoided. Astrid stomped up the steps, her feet like rocks.

The pot was on the kitchen table. It was steaming. The green book was open next to it. For a brief moment, Astrid thought about taking the book with her. She wanted to find out what happened to Heidi in Frankfurt. But then she realized that she couldn't manage any more Heidis for the time being. What she needed now was an explosion. A massive one.

Astrid took the coffeepot and walked past Heidi on the steps outside the house without even glancing at her.

Calmly, and as cool as ice, Astrid emptied out the coffee over what was supposed to be Gunnvald's herb garden. He'd taught her that coffee was especially good for the chives. Heidi didn't say anything: she just sat there on the steps, watching with interest as the little thunderbolt of Glimmerdal placed the coffeepot in the middle of the farmyard, put an enormous charge of firecrackers inside, fished a lighter out of her pocket, lit the firecrackers, and ran for cover behind Gunnvald's wheelbarrow.

Five seconds passed, and then there was such an enormous bang that people ducked right across the glen. It sounded like the sky was falling. Sally had to take one of her pills, Gladiator stopped chewing up at the summer barn, and the terrifying dog crouched down onto his stomach, squeaking like a mouse.

But the blasted coffeepot was still in one piece.

"I'll be back," Astrid told Heidi.

"I have no doubt you will," Gunnvald's daughter replied drily, continuing to drink her coffee as if nothing had happened.

CHAPTER EIGHTEEN

In which life becomes unbearable, and Astrid meets some old friends

"Ah, so you're alive?"

Astrid marched into Gunnvald's room, barely noticing that two other men were asleep in there. Gunnvald looked puzzled, like a big question mark. He had no idea yet. He didn't know that his farm would soon be in the hands of Klaus Hagen. He didn't know that Astrid had been in a fight with his giant daughter, or that she'd ridden her bike down the glen like a lunatic to catch the eleven o'clock boat to town, or that she'd had to beg Able Seaman Jon to let her travel without a ticket, promising that she'd bring him the money on her way home, or that she'd found the way to the hospital in town all by herself, although not before getting lost many times. Gunnvald knew nothing of all this. But there was the little thunderbolt of Glimmerdal, and she was angry: that much he could see.

Astrid paid no attention to the fact that Gunnvald had recently had an operation and was feeling rotten.

"You have a daughter," she started by telling him, in case Gunnvald might have forgotten. "And you've given her your farm. And she's planning to sell it to Mr. Hagen. And she's got a dog that eats people like me, and—"

Astrid stopped just as suddenly as she'd begun, when she saw that Gunnvald's face had gone all pale.

"Did she . . ." Gunnvald began.

"Did she what?"

"Did she come?" Gunnvald whispered.

"Yes," Astrid muttered, scratching her cheek for a moment.

Then neither of them knew what to say. Astrid sank into the chair next to Gunnvald's bed. The two men in the beds next to his snored away. Astrid missed having Gunnvald at home in Glimmerdal. But when she turned to Gunnvald to tell him how terribly she missed him, she saw that he'd hidden his face in his hands and his whole body was shaking. Good heavens! Gunnvald was crying. Astrid was so surprised that she didn't know what to do.

"There's nothing wrong with a little cry," Astrid's mom had told her once.

Astrid remembered when she'd said it. It was when Peter's father had died. Astrid had felt scared because Peter was crying so much.

"When people cry, some of the pain runs out, and then it's easier to help them feel better," her mom had told her.

But Astrid had never seen Gunnvald cry. She didn't know how she could make him feel better. She gently stroked her hand over his uncombed hair. With Gunnvald's hands still covering his face, she took a breath and told him the whole story. She told him about the dog in the kitchen, that Heidi had sat on Astrid's chair, and that her dad had said how much Heidi had grown.

"Seriously, she's huge," Astrid added.

She even told him that she'd fought with Heidi, but she didn't tell Gunnvald it was because Heidi had said that she couldn't care less about him. Astrid couldn't bring herself to say that.

"Do you want me to bring her here?" Astrid asked hesitantly after she'd told him everything.

"No!"

"Since you're her father and everything . . ."

Then Gunnvald seemed to have finished crying.

"Her father? Only when it suited her." His voice was so resentful that Astrid hardly recognized it. "Heidi left me, Astrid! The only reason she's come back now is because I wrote to tell her I was going to die and that she can have the farm. And sell it."

Those last words had a ring to them that Astrid had never heard before. She thought Gunnvald might have thrown a chair then, if he hadn't been lying there with a fractured femur.

"Sell the farm," he said again, shutting his eyes.

A nurse put his head around the door. He said it wasn't visiting hours: Gunnvald needed rest, and the other two men in the room needed to sleep. It would be best if Astrid went home. But Astrid didn't want to go home.

She had no idea what she should do.

"Why did you have to send a letter to that moron of a daughter?" she shouted angrily. "We were getting on fine in Glimmerdal, Gunnvald, weren't we? You could at least have told me she existed! And, by the way, I don't have any money for the boat."

Gunnvald dug out his wallet from the bedside table and gave her the money for the ferry ticket: both the outward leg she hadn't paid for and the return journey. He didn't say a word, but finally he cleared his throat when Astrid shuffled over to the door.

"Astrid?"

"Yes?"

"What does she look like?"

"Who? Heidi?"

Gunnvald nodded.

"She's got a face that would stop a clock. She's the spitting image of you," said Astrid.

Then she slammed the door shut, waking both the snoring men with a start.

*   *   *

Astrid stood there outside the hospital, her hands down by her sides and the money Gunnvald had given her flapping in the wind.

"My life's ruined," she moaned, which was what Auntie Eira said sometimes when things were going against her.

"Your problems are like a fart in the ocean," Auntie Idun would tell her then.

"Well, my fart in the ocean's ruined anyway," Auntie Eira would answer.

Astrid had to smile a little when she thought of her aunts. But then she became serious again. This was no fart in the ocean. If it was, then it had to be the world's biggest fart. A fart the size of a mountain. Heidi, Gunnvald's angry daughter, had come to Glimmerdal. She couldn't care less about Gunnvald, her own father. She'd even left him. And now she had his farm and was going to sell it to Klaus Hagen. What would happen to Gunnvald? Would he have to move down to the elder housing like Nils and Anna? Or to the retirement home in Barkvika? Astrid sat down on the edge of a statue. She had no strength in her legs anymore.

"Astrid!"

A voice came flying through the air like a cannonball. She didn't know anybody in town, did she? But she did! He came running across the parking lot, looking quite dangerous in his baggy pants and his T-shirt with a skull on it and letters dripping in blood.

"Ola!" Astrid shouted happily.

"Do you want me to punch you?" he squealed, clearly remembering how they'd fought the first time they'd met.

All the wonderful memories from February break popped up again from nowhere and danced in the air between them.

"What are you doing here?" Ola asked.

"It's a long story," Astrid said.

"I've got time, and you're paying." He snatched the money from her hand, his eyes sparkling like stars. "It's been umpteen years since we've spent money on anything fun here in town," he proclaimed, happily waving the money aloft.

Astrid wouldn't mind spending some money on something fun. Actually, if truth be told, she felt a burning need to spend money on something fun at that very moment.

They bought ten big custard buns, with loads of custard inside, and then they went to a sort of café, where Ola asked for "Five chocolate milkshakes, please." The lady behind the bar made the thickest milkshake Astrid had ever seen, with vanilla ice cream and real chocolate. She poured it out into five paper cups that were so large Astrid thought they could double as flower vases. She supposed that was how they did things in town.

While Ola led the way through the town, slurping his milkshake like a dehydrated elk, Astrid told him about the coffeepot and the accident and Heidi and the farm. As for their Easter vacation, she added, it was hanging by a thread; that much was clear. The plan had been that Ola, Broder, and Birgitte would come and stay with Gunnvald like last time. That wouldn't happen if Mr. Hagen was going to build another wellness camp up there. Astrid shuddered.

"I've got to think of something clever to make Heidi change her mind!" She looked at Ola in despair.

"Maybe you could dig a trap to maim her? Just a bit?" he suggested.

Astrid had already made a point of stressing how incredibly tall and strong Heidi was—she knew these were details that would interest Ola—so she was quite disappointed by his suggestion.

"I'd have to spend the rest of my life digging to make a hole deep enough. I told you, she's enormous!"

"Peter could do it with his digger."

Astrid shook her head. It was a terrible suggestion, and a bit of a violent one too.

"I know! You can take her hostage!"

"Taking Heidi hostage is just as idiotic as digging a trap," said Astrid.

"You can take her dog hostage," Ola shouted, jumping up and down.

Astrid could almost see the sugar going on a roller-coaster ride around his veins. She shook her head even harder.

"Come on, it's a brilliant idea!" Ola insisted. "You take her dog hostage, and then you tell her she won't get it back until she does what you want! You can lock the dog up in—"

"No," said Astrid. She wasn't going to do anything

that involved dogs. Not under any circumstances.

They'd arrived at the tall block of apartments where Ola's family lived. It had an elevator. Astrid almost felt a bit jealous. Imagine having an elevator you could take every day. She'd have to ask Gunnvald if he could make one for her sometime. Barely had the thought crossed her mind before she sighed. Gunnvald couldn't make an elevator from his hospital bed.

"Astrid!" the others shouted in chorus as they entered the small apartment.

"We've brought milkshakes and custard buns," Ola announced proudly, taking the bag from Astrid.

Everybody was so happy to see her. Astrid stood there, simply smiling back. Birgitte screamed with joy as she came running over, wanting to be lifted up. Their mother stroked Astrid's lion curls, just like Astrid's own mom did. But when they heard that Gunnvald was in the hospital, their smiles vanished.

"You should've told us," their mother said. "Poor Gunnvald. We can go and visit him as often as he can stand."

"I don't know what he can stand now," Astrid mumbled. Then she told the whole story one more time, about Heidi and the farm.

Everybody around the table fell silent when she'd finished.

"Selling the farm is the worst thing anybody could do to Gunnvald," said Astrid. "I think Heidi hates him."

Broder hadn't uttered a word while Astrid was telling the story. He'd put his custard bun down on the table and just sat there, looking at his hands.

"What about Gunnvald, though?" he said after a while.

"What about him?" asked Astrid.

Broder poked his custard bun with one finger. "Has he . . . Has he ever cared about Heidi?"

Astrid looked at Broder. His blond hair had grown longer and hung down a little over his eyes. Had Gunnvald ever cared about Heidi? Astrid remembered what her dad had said about Gunnvald throwing a chair and lighting a bonfire when Heidi left. She remembered how Gunnvald's voice had sounded at the hospital. But most of all, she thought of how Gunnvald had never mentioned a word about Heidi. Ever. Is it possible to care about somebody you never mention?

"I don't know," she whispered eventually.

When she boarded the ferry a little later, Astrid was so deep in thought that she was startled when Able Seaman Jon came to collect her money.

"I spent it all," she admitted, holding her empty hands up to his face. "On milkshakes and custard buns," she added.

"Astrid, you can't keep getting away with not paying every time you take the ferry!" Able Seaman Jon was at the end of his rope.

"You can't throw me in the water. I'm only nine," the little thunderbolt of Glimmerdal protested.

"Really? Can't I?" shouted Jon, grabbing hold of Astrid and lifting her up from her seat as if she were a sack of potatoes.

The other passengers watched in terror as Jon strode the whole length of the cabin with a howling and squirming ticketless passenger over his shoulder. Two young boys, maybe only six years old, hid behind their mother, scared stiff.

"Have mercy!" Astrid begged, twisting and writhing.

"This is what happens to anybody with no ticket," Jon shouted across the cabin. Then he ducked out through the exit, carrying Astrid, his ticket bag, and everything else.

When they got out on deck, he put Astrid down, and they both had to hold on to the railing to stop themselves from collapsing with laughter. They sat out on the windy deck for the rest of the voyage, chatting about this and that while watching the mountains and the shore and the white-capped waves. It cheered them up.

"I know you don't like dogs, Astrid, but one day you should drop by to see Theo at the hair salon. Matisse had five little puppies in early February," Jon told her as they approached land. "And they're growing to be pretty handsome dogs!"

"Really?" Astrid asked. She hadn't heard about the puppies.

"Yup. And guess who's the father?" Jon said proudly.

"Buster?"

"You got it!"

Buster is Able Seaman Jon's dog. Auntie Eira says that he looks like a pile of wet towels and walks like a lame duck.

"It was an accident," Jon explained. "Theo was pretty angry, but how am I supposed to make sure Buster doesn't charm the ladies? Especially exquisite lady show dogs like Matisse."

"No, you're right," Astrid agreed.

"And they're gorgeous puppies," Jon promised her. "You should go and see them. Maybe you'd lose your fear of dogs."

Then Astrid remembered Heidi again. Heidi and the black-haired beast and the farm for sale. Suddenly she felt so downhearted that she sighed out loud.

"I don't like dogs," she told Jon. "Any of them."

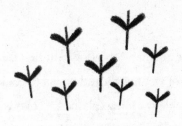

CHAPTER NINETEEN

In which Astrid spies on somebody who disappears

Spring couldn't be stopped, even if everything had changed for some of the people who lived in Glimmerdal. The glen was so full of water bubbling, dripping, and glittering that it was a joy to behold. The meltwater flowed down the mountainsides, and the river roared its deep, throbbing song. Astrid had been falling asleep and waking up to those sounds all her life. The voice of the river was as familiar as her own breathing, always there in the background.

But when Astrid woke up that Sunday morning, she heard the thunderous noises in a new way. She heard the river because she was thinking of Gunnvald, who should have been waking up to the roaring river too, but wasn't there to hear it. Astrid gazed despondently out her attic window. The black dog was tied to the flagpole over at Gunnvald's farm, looking like a little dark blot. It was Heidi living in the house over there now, and soon it would be Mr. Hagen. Soon there might not be any house there at all, only cabins and a wellness retreat.

The evening before, when she'd arrived back from town, Astrid had told her dad everything.

"You've got to talk to Heidi, Dad!"

Her dad, who isn't so fond of talking, squirmed in his chair and said, "Hmm."

"You chicken!" Astrid shouted, stamping her foot.

She regretted saying that right away and buried her head in his stomach, making Snorri quite jealous.

That morning, at her attic window, Astrid felt more lonely than she'd ever felt before. She looked out at the spring scene and thought it would be best to go for a walk.

Under the birch tree below the house, a few snowdrops nodded gently to her as she went past. Astrid nodded back and walked straight over the infield and down the hill. It looked as if the whole glen had kicked off a wintry quilt, she thought.

She was wearing her thick blue sweater for the first time that year. It was the only item of clothing her mom had ever knitted in her entire life, and Auntie Eira had said that it didn't look at all normal, but Astrid loved it.

She stopped by the side of the river to watch the wild water rumbling, thundering, and foaming. The spray clung to her face and made her hair even curlier.

"My river," said Astrid.

There was still a lot of snow here and there, but if she kept to the side where the sun had been burning it off, she could still go for a walk up the glen. Maybe she could even make it all the way up to Glimmerdal Shieling. Astrid trudged on, keeping close to the thundering water. There was only the river, the river, the river. No other sounds. No other thoughts. But then Astrid spotted something on the other bank that made her stop suddenly. At first she thought it was Gunnvald, because it was Gunnvald's jacket. But people who are in the hospital with broken thigh bones don't go for walks.

It was Heidi.

She stood there staring down at the river, exactly like Astrid had just been doing. Her hair waved in the gusting wind. After a while, the tall lady started walking up toward Glimmerdal Shieling too.

Nobody other than the mountains — Cairn Peak and the Glimmerhorn — could see the two girls from the glen, one tall and one small, as they made their way up each side of the thundering river that spring day. Of course, the mountains had seen the little girl in the thick blue woolen sweater all winter, but it took them a while to recognize the other girl, the one in the borrowed jacket and green scarf. When the mountains realized it was Heidi, they smiled to each other, as they remembered her well. But they didn't say a word. They just watched as the two figures made their way up between patches of snow and withered branches on either side of the river.

Heidi stopped twice and looked around, as if she could sense somebody following her. Both times, Astrid hit the ground and lay there, motionless. Her feet were wet from treading through the melting snow, while her lion curls and thick sweater were full of dry leaves. But Astrid hardly noticed.

They were nearly at Glimmerdal Shieling. The old farm buildings had emerged from the snow and were standing there, stretching their old cracked walls in the sun. Astrid waited apprehensively behind a rock. If Heidi was going to the farm buildings, she'd have to cross over the old bridge. But Heidi didn't cross the bridge. She kept on going up her side of the river. Where on earth was she heading? And with no skis? Astrid had never followed the river farther up than Glimmerdal Shieling, as that's where the path turns away from the river and onto the boggy moors.

Astrid thought about it for a moment. It was impossible to go any farther on her side of the river, as there was too much snow and the trees were too densely packed. She'd have to cross over to Heidi's side. The little thunderbolt of Glimmerdal waited for a short time, then scurried over the bridge.

Now she was right behind Heidi. They walked another

couple of hundred meters, and then Heidi finally stopped. They'd come to a small waterfall. Astrid peeked out cautiously from behind a clump of heather.

Heidi stood right by the thundering water, staring down into the surging current. Then suddenly she put one foot in front of the other, and, while Astrid watched her with eyes as round as gooseberries, Gunnvald's daughter jumped straight out into the spring thaw. Astrid almost screamed—her hands raced to cover her mouth.

But Heidi didn't drown! She didn't even fall. The giant woman landed with her right foot on a rock beneath the water. She stood balanced on one leg, as steady as a tightrope walker, sizing up the distance. Then, with the ice-cold river water splashing all the way up her thighs, she swung her arms and took off again. She leaped over onto two other invisible rocks. Her jacket swept out straight behind her like a sail, and her green scarf danced like a kite in the wind. Heidi was running across the surface of the river!

Astrid forgot that Heidi had said she couldn't care less about Gunnvald. She even forgot that Heidi was going to sell the farm to Mr. Hagen. She forgot all about everything, as this was the most dangerous and daring performance Astrid Glimmerdal had ever seen.

"Speed and self-confidence," Astrid murmured breathlessly, filled with a deep sense of awe. If only her aunts could see this!

Astrid was still gaping in admiration when she heard a screech above her head. It was Snorri. He was heading straight for Astrid and her blue woolen sweater. Oh, no! He was going to give her away. Astrid crouched in the heather, trying to make herself invisible.

"*Squaaaaawk!*" went Snorri, making Astrid's eardrums throb.

"Dearest Snorri, you blessed seagull, please go home," she begged him.

Instead, Snorri landed softly on the heather. Soon he'd jump up onto her head, and Heidi would wonder what was so interesting to the seagull behind that bit of heather. Astrid broke into a cold sweat. The last thing she wanted was for Heidi to spot her.

"I'll make you a seagull's castle out of real gingerbread

if you just fly away, my dear, stupid Snorri," she promised him.

He shuffled his feet a little, then he pushed off and climbed into the sky.

"Maybe he's not that stupid after all," she said in surprise.

She lay there for a little longer, and then she peeked out.

Heidi was gone; she'd vanished without a trace. Astrid frowned. None of the trees or the rocks on the other side of the river were big enough for Heidi to have hidden behind them. She hadn't walked off either, as the spring snow was untrodden by human feet both up- and downstream. Had Heidi jumped back over the river? Astrid's stomach was in knots. Was she there? On the same side as her? Or, even worse, what if Heidi had fallen into the river? Astrid thought back to Heidi hopping across; it wouldn't have taken much to slip and fall. Astrid stopped worrying about staying hidden. She leaped down to the water's edge, where she saw something that made the blood in her veins stop flowing.

Heidi's green scarf was hanging from a waterlogged

branch sticking up from the river, in the middle of the strongest rapids.

Later, Astrid was ashamed when she remembered her first thought: *Now that Heidi's drowned, Gunnvald can come home after all*. It was only for a moment, but still. Astrid had no idea that she had such horrible thoughts inside her. Luckily, it wasn't long before her next thought came, which was a kinder one. *No!*

"No!" Astrid shouted, running along the riverbank, scanning the roaring waters desperately. "Heidi! Heidi!"

What could a small person like her do against such a big river? She shouted into the foaming water, the spray lashing at her face. "Heidi!"

Astrid looked around for something that might help her. A tree branch she could push out into the water, another person, anything. She climbed up onto an enormous rock, where she had a good view down over the rapids. She couldn't see anything.

"Heidi!" Astrid yelled again.

"I'm here, Astrid. Over here."

Astrid spun around. Heidi was standing a few meters

behind her. Her jacket was dry. Her hair was dry. Only her pants were wet. She hadn't drowned at all. She was looking at Astrid with her dark eyes, as alive as a woman can be.

"I thought you . . . I saw your scarf . . ."

Astrid couldn't say any more. She was completely drained. Her arms hung by her sides, and the words stuck in her throat. A lopsided smile appeared on Heidi's face.

Then Astrid got angry.

"Take cover!" is what Auntie Idun usually says when she sees Astrid's eyes darken like that.

"You idiot!" Astrid yelled down at Heidi, making the thundering river sound like a game of telephone by comparison. "Do you know how dangerous it is to frighten people like that?"

The little thunderbolt of Glimmerdal was boiling with rage in her blue woolen sweater. But Heidi wasn't fazed.

"How was I to know you were spying on me?" she said calmly.

Astrid spun on her heels and jumped down from the rock furiously. "You would've known if you knew me!" she bellowed. Then she stomped off toward home, the bushes and branches trembling behind her.

Heidi caught up with her after a while. They walked in complete silence. Astrid wasn't planning on looking at that monster of a woman ever again in her whole life. She was so ferociously angry that she was afraid of what she might do. Blinking badgers, what a troll that lady was.

"Sorry, Astrid," said Heidi.

Astrid stopped and turned around. Heidi stopped too. Gunnvald's jacket had slipped down on one of her shoulders.

"I did actually know you were following me, but I didn't mean to frighten you. I'm sorry."

"You knew I was following you?" a surprised Astrid blurted out. "Where were you when I couldn't see you, then?"

"Somewhere secret. You'll have to have a look when summer comes." Then Heidi smiled. Not her lopsided smile, but a real smile. It disappeared behind a cloud in less than a second, but still.

"Nice sweater," she added. Then she walked past Astrid and strode homeward.

"Can't you just forget about selling the farm?" Astrid shouted at Heidi's enormous back.

Heidi didn't answer.

"Heidi!" Astrid ran after her and blocked her path so she'd have to stop whether she wanted to or not. "Gunnvald's got to come home, he—"

"It's none of your business."

Heidi's voice was so harsh that it made Astrid gulp.

"But . . ."

"Do you hear me? The farm's mine, and I'll do what I want with it. That dimwit down at the camp wants to buy it; I want to sell it. End of story."

Heidi forced her way past again.

"Why are you so angry with Gunnvald?" Astrid shouted after her.

She could've bitten off her own tongue. What if Heidi killed her with her bare hands, there below the summit of the Glimmerhorn? Astrid watched, her heart pounding, as Heidi reached out an arm angrily and impatiently. Then Heidi turned around and took a long look at the little girl in the blue woolen sweater.

"Why are *you* so fond of *your* father, Astrid Glimmerdal?" she asked.

CHAPTER TWENTY

In which Heidi starts a seagull massacre, and Astrid hatches a plan

The next day, Heidi started shooting seagulls. But before that battle commenced, Astrid had been to school, and when she'd come home, her dad had made reindeer meatballs for an early dinner. He'd definitely done it to cheer Astrid up. Reindeer meatballs are her favorite.

Astrid's dad had received an e-mail from her mom.

"The sea is rising," her mom had written. "The polar ice is melting and the sea level is rising, but I'll have to pop back home to Glimmerdal soon."

Astrid's mom was doing all she could to stop the seas from rising. It's pollution that makes the ice melt and sea levels rise, but it's still almost impossible to prevent people from doing things that harm the environment.

"If I were the sea, I wouldn't dare rise another centimeter," Auntie Eira had said once when Astrid's mom was telling them all about it. Astrid's mom gets quite worked up when she talks about rising sea levels.

"Do you think she'll be coming home soon?" Astrid asked, her mouth full of reindeer meatballs.

Her dad closed his computer and poured himself an afternoon cup of coffee. "Yes, I think she will," he said.

"Why are *you* so fond of *your* father, Astrid Glimmerdal?" That's what Heidi had asked her the day before. Astrid chewed her meatballs. Because he was her dad, she supposed. Because he had a cuddly beard, and because he made reindeer meatballs when she was sad, and because he looked after her. Astrid thought her dad was kind of like the mountains, actually. He was always there. That's why she loved him.

She'd just swallowed her last meatball when they heard a bang.

There didn't use to be so many seagulls in Glimmerdal.

Their numbers had been growing over the years. Snorri was certainly not the only one anymore. Now there were lots of them making a racket, especially when the garbage truck came to pick up the trash. Then Astrid remembered it just so happened to be trash-collection day.

Heidi clearly didn't like trash-collection day. Astrid looked straight across the glen and saw, to her horror, that their new neighbor was standing with Gunnvald's shotgun in her hands, shooting down seagulls as if they were clay pigeons.

"You must be joking!"

Astrid ran out and jumped on her bike. She didn't take her helmet this time so that Snorri wouldn't follow her, but he did anyway. Stupid creature!

"Go home, you twerp! She'll kill you," Astrid yelled, waving him away.

It was hard to ride like that, with a seagull over her head, one hand on the handlebars, and a crazy armed woman very close by. Down near the river, her bike slipped on the dry grit. Astrid landed on the road, flat on her face. Ow! Her knee was bleeding like anything. Angry and agitated, she left her bike lying there with its wheels spinning and hobbled up the hill.

Heidi was just aiming at another seagull when the familiar red lion curls came into view.

"Stop that right now!" Astrid shouted.

Heidi fired, and another seagull plummeted to the ground. She was a good markswoman. There were already four dead seagulls lying around the farm. Snorri landed on Astrid's shoulder, and she grabbed hold of his legs.

"I won't shoot your seagull, if that's what you're afraid of," said Heidi, starting to gather up the carcasses.

"You mustn't shoot any seagulls!" Astrid said furiously. "Those might be Snorri's aunts, for all you know!"

She looked around in desperation while trying to shield Snorri from the horrific sight.

Heidi didn't care. She stole a glance at Astrid's knee before picking up the last dead seagull. Astrid remembered the last time she'd bled. It was after the fight with Ola. It was Gunnvald who'd bandaged her up then. Now she was standing there bleeding more badly than ever before, and Heidi didn't even mention it.

As Gunnvald's door slammed shut, Astrid realized that there was no other way. She'd have to talk to Mr. Hagen.

Mr. Hagen was quite startled when he saw who it was stepping into his reception. He hadn't seen Astrid up close since the day he'd thrown out those three children and their mother back in the winter. When he remembered that day, and how sad Astrid had been, he had to clear his throat.

"Hello," said Astrid.

She sighed so heavily that Mr. Hagen had to take a second look at her.

"Have you hurt yourself?" he asked when he saw the bloodstained hole in her pants.

Astrid shook her head. "Well, maybe a little, actually."

Mr. Hagen thought for a moment, then he beckoned her over behind the desk and took out a first aid kit. Astrid sat there on his chair, stunned, with her pant leg rolled up, while he cleaned away the blood and the pieces of grit, and then stuck on some bandages with amazing precision. Astrid had never had such straight bandages before.

"There," said Mr. Hagen when he'd finished, waving her back up from the chair.

"Thank you," said Astrid. "Hey, Klaus, I was wondering whether you might do me a favor."

"What kind of favor?" the camp owner asked her skeptically.

"I was wondering whether you could forget about buying Gunnvald's farm."

Mr. Hagen slammed the first aid kit shut. "It seems like you get to decide quite a lot of things around here, Asny."

"Astrid," she corrected him.

"Astrid. But this is none of your business. This is *my* business. I'm running a vacation camp, and I need to make money from it. Now I've been offered a fantastic plot that's closer to the mountains than this site here, has a better view, and offers considerable opportunities for the further overall development of Hagen's Wellness Retreat. You bet I'll be buying it!"

Astrid stamped her foot, unrolling her rolled-up pant leg. "It's Gunnvald's farm!" she protested.

197

"It's a perfect plot for some cabins, that's what it is,"
Mr. Hagen said firmly. "I have great plans for Glimmerdal,
Asny. The farm up there is a gold mine. I'd be an idiot not
to buy it."

"But don't you make enough money already?"

Mr. Hagen's jaw dropped wide open, and he roared with
laughter. Astrid had never heard him laugh before.

"It's a good thing you don't run a business, my dear," he
chortled. "You can never make enough money. You must
never settle for what you have. Ever. If you do that, well,
then you've lost."

As Astrid stood there in front of the rich man, she
pictured giving him a thump on the head. Homes, friends,
dads, moms, fiddle music, the mountains, the river,
rising sea levels: those things were important. Not money.
You didn't even need money to take the ferry. Astrid
remembered the time she'd broken the window and how
Mr. Hagen had taken out the money and given her back
the box. What a prize twerp.

* * *

As Astrid disappeared through the gate, with the world's straightest bandages, Mr. Hagen stood by the window, smiling and shaking his head. Maybe he thought he'd finally gotten the better of the little thunderbolt of Glimmerdal.

If so, he was sorely mistaken.

CHAPTER TWENTY-ONE
In which Astrid can't reveal what's going on

Astrid sat behind the washing machine. She'd just spoken with Gunnvald on the phone. She'd told him about the sheep and how spring was going, but it made no difference, no matter what she said. Gunnvald just grumbled in reply. When Astrid told him about Heidi jumping over the river, Gunnvald said he had to hang up. He couldn't bear hearing about her. Astrid thought it was as if Gunnvald were withering away. Big, strong Gunnvald. She missed him so much now that she didn't know what to do, so she cried her eyes out quietly behind the washing machine. Ugh, how she hated Heidi. She hated her something awful.

Astrid looked at the phone, thought about it for two seconds, and then dialed another number.

"Ola, is that you?" Astrid was whispering. It was best to keep her dad out of it so he wouldn't have to share any of the guilt.

"Of course it's me. Why are you whispering?" Ola asked.

Astrid curled herself up even tighter behind the washing machine. "Can you skip school tomorrow and take the boat here?" she asked him quickly.

"Yup," said Ola.

It certainly was wonderful to have people like Ola, who never think before they do something wrong.

"Great. I'll meet you at the wharf at quarter to eleven."

"But Astrid, I don't have any money."

"Just tell Able Seaman Jon that I sent you. I've got to hang up now."

"Wait!" said Ola. "What are we going to do?"

Astrid bit her lip and peered out from behind the washing machine. Snorri was at the door, looking at her suspiciously.

"We're going to carry out your terrible plan," she whispered. "We're going to kidnap Heidi's dog."

201

*　　*　　*

Astrid's stomach ached when she woke up the next morning, but she went on with her usual routine. She spread some fish roe on her bread, chatted about this and that with her dad, brushed her teeth, swung her backpack on, and ran at full speed to the bridge, where the little school bus, with Lise behind the wheel, was waiting for her. But when they got down to where the other houses were and Lise signaled to turn onto the main road to Barkvika, Astrid said, "Thanks very much, but I'll be getting off here today."

Lise turned around in her comfy driver's seat. She had a questioning look in her eyes. "Aren't you going to school?"

"No, thanks, not today."

"Are you ill?"

"No."

"Are you going to the dentist's?"

"No."

"Are you skipping?"

"It depends how you look at it," Astrid reasoned.

Lise stopped the bus altogether, but she didn't open the door. She was a school bus driver, she said, and it was her

202

job to take children to school, whether they wanted to go or not. She wondered if Astrid had thought what Dagny would say about this.

If Astrid was honest, she couldn't give a hoot what Dagny would say about it. She went right up to Lise. "This is the first and last time in the history of the world that I'll skip school. I promise." She held out her hand seriously.

"Off you go, then, you little thunderbolt." Lise sighed, pressing the button to open the door.

Astrid would wish later that Lise had never opened that bus door.

"The man on the boat said he was going to swab the decks with you," Ola announced as he came bounding down the gangway in his baggy pants. "He says the ferry's going to go broke thanks to you."

"When I'm older and rich from making sleds, I'll pay it all back," Astrid explained.

They had to walk up the glen along the bank of the river so nobody would see them. It took a while. Ola's pants got soaking wet around his ankles, but he didn't complain.

He kept talking nonstop about everything under the sun.

"Wow, it looks totally different here in the spring, doesn't it?!"

Astrid was only half listening. What was she even thinking? Why did she never, ever learn?

The biggest challenge would be sneaking past Sally's house without being seen. Auntie Eira had shown Astrid that there was a way around the back of the green-painted house that meant you didn't have to walk on the road. There was a hole in the enormous hedge of dog rose plants. But you had to put up with getting a few scratches from the thorns. It was unavoidable.

"It's a route to be used only in emergencies," Auntie Eira would always say.

"And since Eira's life is mainly made up of emergencies, she normally takes the route through the rosebushes," Auntie Idun would add.

It was an emergency now. Astrid and Ola crawled silently through Sally's rosebushes, picking up some decent scratches on the way. Then they scurried over the bridge like two crazed rabbits. Astrid felt sick. She didn't know whether it was her fear of dogs or the idea of kidnapping, but she'd never felt so terrible.

"So are you a total chicken around dogs?" Ola asked.

"Yes."

"You've got to be the bravest person I know, then, if you're planning to kidnap a dog even though you're scared of them."

"I'm not *that* brave," said Astrid.

"Am I the one who's going to kidnap it?"

Astrid nodded, and Ola shrugged. He had no problems with kidnapping. You would've thought it was the kind of thing he got up to every day.

They crawled all the way up the hill to Gunnvald's house, keeping behind the stone wall. When Ola eventually saw the dog, he realized why Astrid was as white as a sheet. The dog's fur glistened in the sun, and they could hear him growling all the way from where they were hiding.

"Wow," he whispered. "If I had a dog like that, nobody would ever dare beat me up."

The plan was simple. They had to stay behind the stone

wall and wait until they saw Heidi head up into the mountains or into the barn or down to the camp or wherever. Then they would rush over to the flagpole, untie the dog, and take him with them over to Astrid's farm, where they'd put the dog in the woodshed. Astrid hadn't decided precisely how they'd deal with the ransom demand yet. She'd had enough to think about just with the dog.

"We can write a note," said Ola. "We'll cut out letters from a newspaper and glue together a message on a piece of paper: 'Give the farm back to Gunnvald or we'll take out your dog.'"

"We're not going to 'take out' any dogs," Astrid argued. "We'll just keep him until she gives in."

"We could still write that we're going to take him out, even if we're not really going to do it," Ola insisted.

"No!" said Astrid.

"Honestly, you don't know much about kidnapping and ransom, Astrid. Have you got rubber gloves? We'll look like real amateurs if we leave fingerprints on the note."

It was a good thing they still had a few plans to make, as ages passed without Heidi going anywhere. Ola had started a long lecture about balaclavas and machine guns when they finally heard the door. Astrid's heart almost stopped beating. Great Gunnvald, now it was for real.

Heidi went over to the flagpole and gave the dog some food and water. Behind the wall, two pairs of eyes were following her every step.

"She's massive!" Ola whispered, clearly impressed.

Then they heard her phone ring. Heidi leaned against the flagpole as she answered it. "Yes, I've spoken to the lawyer; he . . . No, we can sort that out tomorrow. . . . Six o'clock? Yes, that'll be . . . No, I'll be going back to Frankfurt, so I'd like to get it all sorted . . . What was that? . . . Asny?"

Astrid stared at Ola, her mouth wide open. It had to be Mr. Hagen. They were talking about her! Astrid heard Heidi snicker. Were they laughing at her in her own glen? Astrid had a good mind to climb over the wall and put a stop to it.

"Was it yesterday she came by?" Heidi asked.

Astrid looked at Ola, flabbergasted. Those two terrible people were talking about her as if she were just a little fart!

But Heidi had stopped laughing. Now she was quite

short and surly with Mr. Hagen. When the call was finished, she stared out into space.

"What a twerp," she muttered. Then she stuffed her phone in her pocket and disappeared into the barn.

"Now!" said Ola, leaping over the stone wall. Astrid saw him running toward the dog. He wasn't scared in the slightest. His sleek hair danced in the sun.

Astrid suddenly felt bad. If anything happened to Ola, she would never forgive herself. How could she ever have thought about being such a coward! Imagine calling one of her best friends and asking him to do something so dangerous that even she wouldn't dare to do it. She hauled herself over the wall and caught up with Ola in two seconds flat.

"I'll do it," she heard herself say.

Then it was as if she'd wandered deep into a tunnel. Her heart was pounding right up in her throat as she untied the dog. Ola was jumping up and down, looking at the barn and telling her to hurry. But it was as if Astrid were no longer in the farmyard at all. She couldn't hear the dog growling right by her ears. In her head, all she could hear was that old goat-herding lullaby; all she could see was Gunnvald; and all she could smell and taste was hot chocolate made out of real chocolate bars. Nothing else.

She heard the music of Gunnvald's fiddle singing in her head as the beast snapped at her arm. And she could still hear the music as the dog's sharp teeth dug into her skin. Astrid was so afraid that she didn't know where she was, but there was fiddle music in her head, and outside her head there was Ola shouting and the dog snarling.

"Let Astrid go!" Ola howled at the dog, pulling at his collar. "Let her go! Let her go!"

She was going to die! She was sure of it.

Then Heidi came running across the farmyard. She yelled at the dog and hit him until he let go of Astrid's arm with a whimper. The little thunderbolt of Glimmerdal staggered backward and then fell down flat on the ground, her lion curls spread out around her head in a wild fan shape.

The dog whimpered. Astrid whimpered. The sun shone down on them.

"Astrid! Astrid!" Ola shouted frantically. "It was me who was supposed to take the dog!"

"Shush," Heidi scolded him brusquely, crouching down on one knee. She pulled out her phone. "I'm going to call Sigurd," she said. "You'll have to go to Barkvika to get a tetanus injection."

That evening, Astrid's dad sat on the edge of her bed without saying anything. Astrid had a bandage on her arm, but that wasn't why she was crying. She was crying because her life was so miserable. She was crying because Gunnvald was in the hospital and still couldn't come home. She was crying because Heidi was going to sell the farm to Mr. Hagen. And most of all, Astrid Glimmerdal was crying because she was a little girl who couldn't do anything about it.

"Heidi's put down her dog," Astrid's dad said after a while.

Astrid stopped crying and looked at him, terrified. "Did she shoot him?"

Astrid's dad nodded.

Then Astrid flung herself onto her dad's lap and wept even more.

CHAPTER TWENTY-TWO
In which old Nils gets drunk
and says something very true

On her way home from school the next day, Astrid got off the bus by the houses down the glen. She couldn't bear to go home. She didn't want to see Gunnvald's farm that wasn't Gunnvald's farm anymore, and she didn't want to see the flagpole with no dog next to it, thanks to her. And she never, ever wanted to see Heidi again.

But what was she going to do down at the bottom of the glen? Astrid was standing there, feeling downhearted, when she suddenly caught sight of old Nils. He was out for a spin with his walker. For a while, Astrid just stood with her hands behind her back, watching. First, Nils walked straight into the flagpole outside the closed-down snack bar. Then he got his walker untangled and walked slalom-style across the wharf. Astrid could see he was having a funny turn and thought it would be best to take him home so he didn't toddle over the edge of the wharf and drown.

"Come on," she said, taking Nils by the arm.

"It's got a mind of its own," Nils complained, pointing at his walker.

Astrid took baby steps as she walked alongside the old man. When they got to the old ice-cream table, they had to stop for a break.

"Is it true that little Heidi's come home?" Nils asked hazily.

Little wasn't quite the right word, Astrid thought, but she nodded. Horrible Heidi. Then it all came spilling out of her, all the awful things that had happened over the past few days. It was a long and almost endless tale of misery. Nils listened and nodded and said "Hmm." He probably wasn't really listening, Astrid thought.

But when she'd finished, he fumbled around for his

snus and said, "I remember the day she left."

Nils's eyes weren't looking at Astrid or the wharf anymore. It was as if they were looking inside him, back to the old days, back to that time almost thirty years before, when Nils still drove a truck and lived in his own house with Anna, and when Gunnvald still had black hair and was the strongest man in Glimmerdal.

"The day Heidi left, Gunnvald came down to me," said Nils, his voice not as unclear anymore. "I've never seen a more devastated man, Astrid. Gunnvald loved that daughter of his so much that nobody else could understand. And poor Heidi, she was so fond of Gunnvald—"

"She wasn't! She left him!"

Astrid's voice was as angry as Gunnvald's had been at the hospital. Nils maneuvered his horrible snus into place under his lip and chuckled a little.

"That's what Gunnvald says, yes. But it was that awful Anna Zimmermann who was to blame for the whole thing, Astrid. She was the one who took Heidi away. As if she were a package," he added, clearing his throat.

"But Heidi went with her," Astrid said as harshly as before.

With some difficulty, Nils turned around and fixed his blurred eyes on her. "Have you never wanted to go with your mother when she leaves on her expeditions, you little thunderbolt?"

Astrid huddled up on the bench.

Ah yes, those days when Astrid's mom packed her computer and all her important papers into her watertight red bag. Her woolen good-bye pullover that smelled of the ocean. Her dad standing in the doorway with Snorri, looking at Astrid's mom with his lovey-dovey eyes. Her mom's hair when she was just out of the shower, reaching all the way down her back. Astrid always wondered what it was going to be like by the sea, where her mom would unpack her things in a small cabin or on a big boat. And each time she wondered how long it would take for her dad to start looking forward to her mom coming home instead of being sad that she was gone. Astrid could never leave her dad. Or could she? If her mom asked her? If her mom asked if Astrid wanted to come along on an

214

ocean expedition? Wouldn't Astrid go with her then so
she wouldn't have to hang around being motherless
all the time?

"Maybe," she said, looking sadly at old Nils.

"Grown-ups do lots of stupid things, Astrid. I should
know, sitting here drunk on a Wednesday afternoon." He
shook his head at himself. "But there's one important thing
to remember." He turned toward her. *"Nothing is ever the
children's fault."*

Nils tapped Astrid on the knee as he said it, as if
he wanted to leave the words stamped in her mind.
"Nothing – is – *ever* – the – children's – fault."

"What's never the children's fault?" Astrid gasped.

"Anything. All the things grown-ups do wrong." Nils's
voice was clear and certain.

They sat there in silence for a long time. The seagulls
shrieked around them, and the waves lapped beneath the
ferry landing.

"And Gunnvald's never gotten that into his thick head,"
Nils grumbled eventually. "Heidi was only a young girl
back then."

215

"But she went with her," Astrid said again, more softly this time.

"What else was she to do? Heidi was a fiend at the fiddle. She knocked spots off her father. When Anna Zimmermann found out, she went ahead and decided that Heidi should go to Germany and learn properly. Just you ask Gunnvald if he ever called his daughter after she left. Or if he sent her letters, or if he went to visit her. You ask Gunnvald about that, Astrid."

Astrid huddled up even more on the bench. "Did he?"

"Ask Gunnvald." Nils snuffled.

Astrid thought about the time Gunnvald had thrown a chair at the wall because her uncle had asked if Heidi was ever going to come back.

"I've probably said too much. You'd better take me home, otherwise my dear little Anna will hit me over the head with a rolling pin," Nils mumbled, scratching his head anxiously and spitting out a disgusting glob of snus.

Astrid was very deep in thought. She'd dropped Nils off at the elder housing and was shuffling back up Glimmerdal.

216

But then she was torn out of her thoughts. There was Theo, standing outside his hair salon, smoking.

"Didn't you stop smoking?" Astrid asked him.

"Yes," said Theo, "but Matisse's pups are killing me. It's that mongrel of Able Seaman Jon's that's the father. They just don't look right," he complained crossly. "Now they're starting to grow and they're getting restless."

Astrid couldn't cope with any more problems, and certainly not any that were canine related, but Theo dragged her into the salon.

"There! Look!" he announced.

Matisse, Theo's petite white show dog, was lying in a large basket, and crawling around her were five puppies that looked slightly odd, to put it mildly. Astrid wanted to run away, but before she knew it, she was standing there with one of the small spotted creatures in her hands.

"Take him!" said Theo. "You can have him, Astrid."

Astrid was terror stricken and held the puppy at arm's length. He was tiny and kicked his legs in the air.

"Take him," Theo urged again.

"I don't want to!"

She looked at Theo in panic, but just as he was about to take the puppy back, she held the sweet little dog close to her. His heart was thundering like a tractor inside his tiny soft body.

"All right, I'll take him," she whispered. "Thank you."

CHAPTER TWENTY-THREE

In which Heidi and Astrid engage in a kind of trench warfare that not even Mr. Hagen can disrupt

The afternoon sun was resting on Storr Peak when Astrid finally arrived. Her legs shook as she crossed the farmyard and walked past the flagpole and up the steps to the house. The puppy had been whimpering a bit on the way there. So had Astrid, if truth be told.

She knocked on the door. Nobody answered. Cautiously Astrid tried the door handle. Locked. She went around the side of the house and peered into the kitchen. Heidi's back was covering half the window. When Astrid knocked on the window, Heidi turned around and looked at her grumpily, then pulled the curtains shut.

"I'm not leaving!" Astrid shouted. "I'm going to stay here until you open up, got it?"

Back on the doorstep, she took out her woolly hat and put it under her bottom. You could catch a chill if you sat on cold stone steps for too long—and Astrid was planning on sitting there for as long as she had to.

"There, there, little pup, we're just going to wait here." She comforted the dog, stroking it with trembling hands. "I've got to get rid of you, you see."

Thus began a real trench war in the glen. On either side of Gunnvald's door sat a stubborn-as-nails girl from Glimmerdal, waiting with clenched teeth. Heidi was waiting for Astrid to leave; Astrid was waiting for Heidi to open up.

When Astrid had been sitting on the steps for over two hours and the time was half past six, Mr. Hagen came storming up to the farm, his car brakes screeching.

"Have you locked her inside?" he asked Astrid.

"I'm the one who's locked out," Astrid explained.

Mr. Hagen asked Astrid to move. Astrid didn't move.

"Adelheid Zimmermann! This is Mr. Hagen!" he shouted.

"We had an appointment at six o'clock!"

Astrid lowered her head, hiding a smile behind her jacket collar.

"Wipe that smile off your face, Asny," Mr. Hagen snapped, clearly annoyed. "If you think you can ruin this deal, then you're wrong. Adelheid Zimmermann!"

He walked around the side of the house and knocked on the kitchen window. He knocked hard and kept knocking for a while.

But there wasn't a sound from inside Gunnvald's house, and eventually Mr. Hagen had to leave. He spat out some spectacularly bad words about all the preposterous women in this glen and roared away in his big car. It was so gloriously quiet when he'd left that Astrid sighed with happiness. She leaned against the door frame and closed her eyes.

She must have nodded off for a while, as suddenly there was somebody gently stroking her cheek.

"Don't you want to come home, Astrid?"

It was her dad. He looked at the dog and at the closed door. Astrid shook her head.

221

"Fair enough," he said.

He went, and when he came back half an hour later, he'd brought a flask of soup for Astrid, a bowl with some cold food for the puppy, and some warm blankets.

"You might have a long night ahead of you," he said, nodding in the direction of the closed door. "Believe me."

He tapped Astrid's nose with his finger and smiled as he wandered off back down the hill.

"That's my dad," Astrid whispered softly, her eyes following him all the way home.

It was during that long night that Astrid Glimmerdal lost her fear of dogs. It just wasn't possible to sit there all night being scared of a strange, whimpering puppy. When Astrid realized he was freezing, she even tucked him under her sweater, with only the dog's head sticking out of her collar. His soft coat tickled against her skin.

She smiled. "I've got two heads."

Astrid had slept outdoors many, many times with her aunts in the summer. Often they just went over to the edge of the forest, or down to the swimming hole by the river, and rolled out their ground mats. When darkness fell and the birds went quiet, the ceaseless thundering of the river was the only sound to be heard in Glimmerdal. It was the best way to fall asleep. Astrid leaned against the door frame and pretended it was a summer evening. A gentle night breeze stroked her cheeks. And when her dad switched off the lights on the other side of the glen, Astrid fell asleep too.

At three o'clock in the morning, she woke up freezing. Rain was pouring down! She was absolutely soaked, even through her sweater to where she was holding the puppy.

"Heidi, you've got to open up before we catch something!" Astrid shouted drowsily.

Nobody opened up.

Now Astrid really was tired *and* cold! And there was something else she'd started thinking about: her promise to Lise that she'd never ever in the history of the world skip school again. What would she do if Heidi still hadn't opened up in the morning? She would have to go to school.

"Heidi! Please!"

No reaction. You would've thought Heidi was dead or

something. To console herself, Astrid started singing the old goat-herding lullaby. She let out verse after verse there on the doorstep. And when she finished, she started all over again.

Nobody can sing "Bluey, Billy Goat of Mine" like I can, Astrid thought happily. *And nobody can play it as well as Gunnvald,* she added.

No sooner had she thought that than she heard a fiddle playing.

Astrid felt scared. She'd read the story about "The Little Match Girl," the poor girl who froze to death on New Year's Eve. The first sign that she was almost dead was when she started imagining things that weren't there.

"Am I freezing to death? How else can I be hearing Gunnvald playing his fiddle?"

Astrid straightened her back and shook her head. The tune "Bluey, Billy Goat of Mine" was coming from behind the closed door. And now Astrid could hear that it wasn't Gunnvald playing. The notes were completely different. It was as if the fiddle were toying with the tune and playing something that resembled it but wasn't quite the same after all. Astrid was mesmerized. So was the dog. He looked around in confusion from the collar of Astrid's sweater; he couldn't understand what was going on.

When the music died down, Astrid got to her feet and leaned with her ear against the door. Suddenly, there was somebody opening the door, and Astrid fell into the hallway like a sack of potatoes. She was just able to turn enough in midair to land on her back so she wouldn't squash the puppy into a puppy pancake.

There she lay, as wet as a sheep left to graze outdoors all year round. Above her stood Heidi, a fiddle in her hands. She didn't say a word.

CHAPTER TWENTY-FOUR

In which Astrid gets to hear the end of the book, and Heidi reveals more

I've brought you a new dog," Astrid said as she lay there on the floor.

Heidi looked at the little head peeping out from Astrid's sweater. "That's the ugliest dog I've ever seen in my entire life," she said.

Astrid nodded. "But he doesn't bite."

Heidi reached out a hand and helped Astrid up without saying any more.

A little later, Astrid was sitting on the sofa, wearing one of Heidi's woolen sweaters. It was like a big warm nightie. Her wet clothes were hanging to dry by the stove. She'd been given some hot chocolate in her own special mug. Some crazy hot chocolate made out of dark chocolate with chili: Astrid had never tasted anything like it.

She plunged her head down into the enormous mug, and when she came back up, she cleared her throat. "I'm so sorry about what happened with your dog, Heidi."

Heidi brushed it off as if it were nothing. "That dog was vicious. I should've shot him ages ago. I just couldn't bring myself to do it. I got him from a friend who died, and, well, he's been living at my farm for—"

"You have a farm?" Astrid asked her, stunned.

Heidi nodded. "I've got a farm in eastern Norway, but I'm only there from time to time, and I don't manage it myself."

"Because you live in Frankfurt, right?" Astrid said.

"Well, yes, I own a town house there now too, since Anna died."

"And that's where you live?"

"Yes, when I'm not in my apartment in Hong Kong."

"Hong Kong?"

"Or in Portugal."

227

Astrid's jaw dropped. "Are you rich?"

Heidi laughed. This time it was a beautiful laugh. "Yes, unfortunately I am," she said. She turned her mug around in her hands and stretched out one of her enormous legs on the kitchen floor.

"Have you been to Greenland?" Astrid asked her.

"No, I've never been there," said Heidi.

"Mom has. She works there."

"Really?"

It was wonderful for Astrid to talk about her mother with somebody who wanted to listen. Astrid told Heidi about the rising sea levels, about her mom's research, and about what it was like in Greenland, the way her mom had spoken about it in e-mails and on the phone.

"She's coming home soon, because she's missing Glimmerdal now," Astrid finished.

Heidi smiled a little. "Yes, it's hard to forget Glimmerdal as you travel around the world."

"Do you miss Glimmerdal, then? When you're traveling around the world?" Astrid asked.

"Yes, you miss it then," said Heidi. "You long to go back

228

to Glimmerdal so much it makes your stomach hurt."

"Every day?" Astrid asked, horrified.

"Every day."

Astrid had never seen anybody change from smiling to serious as quickly as Heidi. The tall lady got up suddenly and stiffly. She went over to the stove, mixed in the thin skin that had formed on the rest of the hot chocolate, then turned back toward Astrid.

"You know Gunnvald quite well, don't you?" she asked.

Astrid nodded.

"Does he ever mention me?"

"Huh?" said Astrid, wishing that Heidi had asked something else.

"Has Gunnvald ever mentioned my name?"

Oh, how Astrid wished she could say yes. What a fool Gunnvald had been, never saying a single word about having a daughter. Astrid stared down into her brown hot chocolate with red pieces of hot chili bobbing up and down.

"Has he?" Heidi asked again.

"No," Astrid mumbled.

They fell silent. Astrid squirmed a little on the sofa,

wishing that it weren't all so difficult. Then she spotted the green book on the kitchen table.

"You're almost like the Heidi from the book: you've got the same name, and then you both went to Frankfurt."

"Yes." Heidi drummed her fingers on the green book, and then she said that Gunnvald used to read to her.

"Did he?" Gunnvald had never read anything to Astrid.

"He did, and this was my favorite book. We must have read it thirty times," said Heidi. "We used to pretend that I was Heidi from the book and that Gunnvald was my grandfather. Sally down by the bridge: she was Peter the goatherd's old grandmother. And Sigurd, your father: he was Peter."

"Dad pretended he was Peter the goatherd?" Astrid asked in disbelief.

"You bet he did," said Heidi. "We used to run around the mountains every day. For my eighth birthday, Gunnvald bought us two goats, so we could play it for real."

Astrid almost felt a little jealous as she sat there. She wished there were a book about a girl called Astrid too.

"What happens to Heidi? I haven't finished reading

the book. You and the dog came and interrupted me."

Heidi tapped her finger on the book again, then she picked it up and sat down on the sofa. "I can read you a bit, if you want."

There was some discussion and they had to flick back and forth a little so they could check how far Astrid had gotten, but eventually they worked out that she must have been on page 113, at the part where Heidi was up in the church tower in Frankfurt, looking for the mountains.

It was a bit strange to start with, sitting there and being read to by a lady with whom Astrid was really tremendously angry, but both Astrid and Heidi eventually got swept up in the story, forgetting that it was the middle of the night and they were enemies.

The Heidi from the book was extremely unhappy in Frankfurt. She missed home so much that she couldn't eat, and then she started sleepwalking, so people thought the old house was haunted. It was the kind doctor who finally found out how much Heidi was hurting, by which time Heidi had almost died of sorrow and homesickness.

"Can you really die of homesickness?" Astrid asked, shocked.

Heidi wasn't sure. She thought the author might have been exaggerating a little. But if the Heidi from the book had practically stopped eating, then she probably was quite weak. Anyway, the doctor told Mr. Sesemann, the father of Clara, the girl in the wheelchair, that there was only one remedy for Heidi: she'd have to go back home to her grandfather and to the mountains. Right away.

"Yes!" Astrid shouted.

It was almost six in the morning by the time they finished the first part. By that point, Heidi had come home, all was well, and everybody was happy.

"This is the best book I've ever listened to!" Astrid said in all seriousness. "Don't you think the place up there where the grandfather lives sounds a bit like Glimmerdal Shieling?"

Heidi nodded.

Astrid looked down at her toes sticking out of the woolen sweater. There was something she had to ask, but it was a bit difficult.

232

"Why didn't you come back home to Gunnvald?" she whispered eventually.

A long moment passed before Heidi said anything.

"Gunnvald never asked me if I wanted to," she finally replied.

Astrid slowly sat all the way up, gazing at Heidi with wide eyes. "He didn't?"

Heidi shook her head. "When Anna came to take me away, I kept on pretending I was the Heidi from the book. You know, it was almost like when Aunt Deta came, even though it was my mother. To start with, it was exciting in Frankfurt. I got to play the fiddle every single day with a really good teacher, and Anna took me everywhere with her. I had been missing her, you know."

Astrid nodded. She could sympathize with that.

"But I was sure that Gunnvald would call soon and say I could come home to Glimmerdal," said Heidi. "I only had to stay in Frankfurt for a while, I thought, like Heidi does in the book. I longed to come back here. I longed to go back to Sigurd the goatherd, to the mountains, to the river, to the sheep . . . And to Gunnvald.

Most of all to go back to Gunnvald. And the more I missed Glimmerdal, the more I thought I was like the Heidi in the book. In the end I couldn't take it anymore and secretly called home. I called several times, but nobody answered."

Heidi went quiet for a long while.

"Gunnvald never called me, Astrid. Not once. He just stopped being my father."

Astrid Glimmerdal sat there on the sofa, wearing the enormous woolen sweater and feeling like something had collapsed inside her. How could Gunnvald have been like that? Gunnvald, who had always been so kind to Astrid—how could he have done that to Heidi? Didn't he know how fond people can get of their fathers? Astrid turned around and buried her face in one of the cushions on the sofa. She didn't want Heidi to see her crying.

Astrid's dad didn't say very much when they arrived. He just gave them a little smile from behind his beard and made some breakfast. When Astrid staggered off to school, she knew three things. She knew that her dad and

234

Heidi were still sitting in the kitchen, drinking coffee. She knew that Heidi wasn't going to sell the farm to Mr. Hagen. And she knew it felt as if something had died inside her.

CHAPTER TWENTY-FIVE
In which Astrid is reacquainted with an old man

"Triplets!" Astrid shouted, jumping up and down.

"You're turning into quite the farmer," her father mumbled drowsily.

He prefers it when the ewes have twins. When they have triplets, there's so often some kind of trouble, and before you know it, you've got a little bottle lamb on your hands. Bottle lambs have to be hand-fed with a baby's bottle, which is a lot of work. That's why Astrid's dad prefers twins, but Astrid loves bottle lambs, so she was hoping there would be heaps of them causing trouble.

It was nonstop now, day and night. Astrid's dad and Heidi were on lambing duty on their respective farms and could hardly get any sleep. Peter did a shift every now and then so they could snatch forty winks. Astrid begged to be allowed to help out too, but her dad was strict about it. She had to go to school and had to sleep at night.

"How am I supposed to become a farmer if I can't stay up at night?" Astrid shouted angrily.

Astrid's dad thought she'd get on fine anyway; and besides, nine-year-olds were only allowed an all-nighter once a month—that was just the way it was—and Astrid had already used up her quota on Heidi's doorstep.

As for Heidi, Astrid had grown to like her. She knew how to play the fiddle. She knew how to make strange food. She knew how to deliver lambs. She knew how to jump over rivers. And she knew how to make Astrid's dad laugh out loud. Astrid was quite astonished when she heard him. Her dad had spent the previous few days training Heidi, as it was a long time since she had done any lambing. On one of those days, when Astrid came into their barn, she found her dad and Heidi each hanging over the edge of one of the pens, laughing so much they had hiccups, while the ewes and the puppy stared at them as if they were aliens.

"What are you laughing at?" Astrid asked, but neither her dad nor Heidi knew. They were just laughing.

Astrid was starting to realize that her dad and Heidi had been almost like brother and sister once upon a time. She'd asked her dad all about it over the past few days, and he'd told her about how they used to play together, about the time they'd spent in the mountains, and about how bossy Heidi used to be back then. Astrid's dad and his younger brothers always had to do what she said.

Astrid and her dad had certainly talked about many things recently, but there was one thing Astrid couldn't bring herself to talk about, and that was Gunnvald. Every time her dad tried to ask Astrid if she wanted to visit him, Astrid started discussing something else.

One day, Gunnvald even called and asked for her.

"He wants to speak with you, Astrid," her dad said, holding out the phone.

Astrid stood there for a moment, looking at the telephone, and then she ran outside. She ran and ran until her mouth tasted of blood. She didn't want to talk to Gunnvald.

*   *   *

Astrid's dad used some hay to wipe the worst of the blood and mess off the newly born triplets.

"Dad, why don't you get some sleep tonight, and I can stay here?" Astrid begged. "I can manage!"

"I know you can manage, but you're not allowed."

"But you're so tired."

"I'm never tired," her dad lied as he climbed out of the pen. He ruffled her hair. "It's reindeer meatballs for dinner tonight."

"I don't need cheering up," Astrid said, also lying. "I'm never sad."

Her dad put his hand on her shoulders, below her neck, and they went out into the farmyard and the sunlight. Then both Astrid and her dad suddenly stopped and stared ahead.

Auntie Eira once said that nobody in the world can shout "Mom!" like Astrid can. "You shout it so loud that you make the tree trunks snap all the way down the glen."

Now Astrid found herself doing it again, as there, ahead of them, wrapped in sunlight, stood Astrid's mom. Astrid ran and reached her in just two steps. Her mom's kind arms held her tightly, and her woolen pullover had such a good smell of the ocean that Astrid could've stood there smelling it all day.

"God, how I've missed you," her mom whispered into Astrid's lion curls and into her dad's beard, while Astrid's joyful shout could still be heard dancing among the mountains.

Astrid's mom put down her backpack and her red watertight bag in the hallway and rubbed her nose against Snorri's beak. Then Astrid's dad could finally be a tired dad, and Astrid could finally be a sad Astrid, as Mom was home now. Dear, kind, comforting Mom.

Astrid's dad fell asleep like a baby on the sofa in front of the news. Astrid's mom kissed him on the forehead and put a blanket over him, then she took Astrid with her out into the barn. They sat close to each other as they started the all-night lambing shift, and Astrid talked and talked.

"Gunnvald never called Heidi," she muttered quietly when she'd finished, staring into the darkness of the barn.

"Tomorrow, Astrid, we're going to visit Gunnvald," said her mom.

"No," said Astrid.

"Yes," said her mom.

It's strange, but things tend to turn out the way Astrid's mom says. Astrid thought that must be where she'd gotten it from.

Now Astrid and her mom were standing outside Gunnvald's room. He wasn't at the hospital anymore; he'd gone to a place just outside town where they were teaching him how to walk again. Astrid's heart was pounding as her mom knocked on the door.

"Hello?" they heard a voice say. They walked in and entered a bright, pleasant room.

An old man was sitting in an armchair in the middle of the room.

"Oh, Gunnvald," said Astrid's mom. "What have they done to your hair?"

They'd cut it and combed it, and Gunnvald was unrecognizable. He was pale too, and thin.

Astrid's mom walked straight over to Gunnvald and

messed his hair back up again. They said hello to each other and chatted. Gunnvald told her about his thigh bone and his ankle, and he asked about Greenland and the rising sea levels, but he kept getting distracted and glancing over at Astrid. She stood there, looking down at the ends of her shoes: one was pointing straight forward, while the other was pointing a little out to the side. She didn't want to look at him. She didn't want to be there.

"Astrid?"

She didn't answer. She could feel Gunnvald's eyes on her, and eventually she had to lift up her head and look at him. He didn't look like Gunnvald anymore. His cheeks were hollow. They spent a long time looking at each other like that. Then Gunnvald cleared his throat.

"Astrid, what would I do without you?"

Then the dam burst. Astrid Glimmerdal ran across the room and flung herself around his neck. "You're the biggest fool I know!" she said, sobbing.

He really was. He was big, and he was a fool too. But he was also her best friend, after all, and she'd missed him so much that it was a wonder she hadn't died from it.

"I'm going to get us some Danish pastries," said Astrid's mom.

When they were alone, Astrid sat down in the chair on the other side of the table. She could see that Gunnvald was going to ask about school and the sheep and the snow, but he could save himself the trouble.

"Why did you never call Heidi?"

Gunnvald realized that if he still wanted to have a goddaughter, he'd have to make an effort and give her an answer. He drew a breath and put his hands on his knobbly knees.

"I was angry with Anna Zimmermann, Astrid," he admitted. "First she came along with Heidi and left her with me without asking. Heidi grew up with me, and I grew so fond of her. Then Anna came back and took her away again without asking. And Heidi went with her. She wanted to leave me!"

Gunnvald's face wore a devastated look.

"Nothing is ever the children's fault," Astrid said, showing no mercy.

"No, I know," said Gunnvald.

"Heidi's been longing to come back home her whole life, you know. You were the one who didn't want to have her back."

"But I did!"

"Why didn't you call her and tell her, then?"

Astrid was shouting now. Gunnvald ran his hand through his newly cut hair. It was far too short.

"You don't know what it was like, Astrid. I've spent all these years trying to forget she existed, because—"

"You're not allowed to think like that!" she yelled. "If you're a dad, then you're always a dad! You can't just stop being one if bad things happen."

Gunnvald looked out the window. When he turned back to Astrid, he had tears in his eyes.

Astrid felt so sorry for him. And she felt sorry for Heidi. In her mind, there was one old bag who was worse than anybody, and that was Anna Zimmermann. Imagine ruining something so good the way she had.

Astrid got up and stroked Gunnvald's cheek where a tear had made it wet. "They're doing a good job of shaving you here," she said. "You almost look normal."

244

"Oh, good heavens, how I wish I were in Glimmerdal and didn't have to shave," Gunnvald grumbled.

"Close your eyes," Astrid said.

Then she told him how the trees in Glimmerdal were looking now. There was color on the buds, and the spruce trees smelled wonderful, as did the land. Astrid told him how it smelled when she lay down on her stomach and buried her nose in the waking grass. Meanwhile, the mountains were losing a bit more snow every day, she told him, but there was still enough left for her aunts to go skiing when they came at Easter. That was, if they went up high enough, which of course they would. Aunts like hers could never get enough of going high up into the mountains. Sally was going on about her crocuses every day, which was enough to make anybody crazy, so Gunnvald should be glad he had to stay in town for his physical therapy. But Gunnvald would soon be able to come back and sit on his old stone steps. The steps were so warm in the midday sun now that you could sit there without getting a cold backside. And the roads were all free of snow, but they were still wet. Only the bridge was dry, and there was grit on it that made people skid on their bikes.

"And the river," said Astrid. "The river is thundering away as ever. You know what it's like, don't you?"

Of course Gunnvald knew what it was like. He sighed as he sat there with his eyes closed.

"Astrid, can you bring me my fiddle the next time you come?" he asked. "If it's not going to be too long a wait until next time, I mean," he added.

"You won't have to wait too long," Astrid promised, shaking hands on it.

Gunnvald gently squeezed her hand. There was something he was about to ask. Astrid waited. Nothing came.

"What is it, you stubborn old mule?" she asked eventually.

Gunnvald took a deep breath. "Is it true that Heidi missed home?"

That was when Astrid realized that Gunnvald still couldn't believe it. She sat back down in her chair and looked at her skinny best friend with his hair cut so short.

"Yes," Astrid said sincerely. "She missed home every day, Gunnvald. So much it made her stomach hurt."

MUSIC

Glimmerdal has a special sound. If you listen carefully, you'll hear it. It's the sound of the pounding river. It's the sound of the wind making the spruce trees whisper and the mountains sigh. It's the sound of the birds too. And sometimes, if you're lucky, you'll hear other sounds mixed in as well. Sometimes it's the notes of a red-haired girl singing, or an old troll playing his fiddle.

And every now and then, if you're really lucky, you can hear something that's nothing like anything else: miracle music.

CHAPTER TWENTY-SIX

In which Heidi shows Astrid something really fantastic

Y ou've got a great mother," said Heidi.

She and Astrid were on their way up toward Glimmerdal Shieling.

Astrid smiled. She liked it when people said nice things about her mom. Not everybody did. Some people thought she should spend a little less time thinking about the sea.

"What about your mother?" Astrid asked.

Heidi laughed a little. "My mother was good at playing the fiddle," she said.

"Did you love her?"

"Surely everybody loves their mother," said Heidi. "But I suppose I was normally more angry at her."

"So was Gunnvald," said Astrid.

It was a strange walk they were on, Astrid thought. She'd gone over to see Heidi and told her that Gunnvald had asked for his fiddle, and then, instead of giving her the fiddle, Heidi had packed it in its case and slipped it in her orange backpack. Then she'd told Astrid to go home and put on some sturdier shoes.

"I've got something to show you," she'd said.

So now they were on their way up to Glimmerdal Shieling with a fiddle in Heidi's backpack.

"Oh, I'm looking forward to Easter so much!" said Astrid, dancing around Heidi's legs.

Just think: then Gunnvald would be coming home, and Ola, Broder, Birgitte, and their mother would be coming too. It was certainly going to be full at Gunnvald's farm this year. Astrid wondered what Heidi would think of Ola and Broder. Of course she'd already met Ola that time they tried to steal her dog, but Astrid didn't want to think about that. She looked ahead up the path.

Glimmerdal Shieling had to be the best place on earth: Astrid was sure of it.

"We've got to come up and spend the night here this summer, Heidi!" she said excitedly when they spotted the old buildings. She was about to go over the bridge, but Heidi signaled that they were heading farther up.

Then Astrid suddenly realized that they weren't going to the old mountain farm, but to the waterfall where she'd seen Heidi walk across the river.

"Remember that my legs aren't as long as yours," she warned Heidi as she pictured the enormous leaps Heidi had taken last time.

There was less water in the river now, and the invisible rocks that Heidi had jumped across the last time formed a kind of bridge.

"They might be slippery," said Heidi.

"Rocks in the river are always slippery, aren't they?" said Astrid, breathing as much speed and self-confidence into her lungs as possible.

They made it over: first Astrid, with her lion curls dancing in the gusts of wind blowing across the river, and then Heidi with her orange backpack.

"I've never been here before," Astrid told her, looking

253

at the dark solid rocks behind the waterfall.

"I have," said Heidi. "But I've never shown it to anybody. Follow me."

Astrid was so excited that she was fizzing inside. But she couldn't see anything out of the ordinary anywhere.

That soon changed. Heidi walked right up to the waterfall, and then she vanished, as if the rock had swallowed her. There was no visible hole hiding in the shadows, though. Astrid stared, her mouth wide open, then she ran over and reached out her hand. There was an opening between a wet root and the rock face. What on earth? Eagerly Astrid slipped into the dark, narrow space.

Pitch black. She reached her hands out in front of her, but she couldn't feel anything apart from air. Eventually her eyes became used to the dark, and she could see that the hole in the rock went even farther back.

"Heidi?"

"Just keep going straight!" a voice said from somewhere deep inside the rocks.

Astrid groped her way forward, never having to crouch. The sound of the thundering river grew quieter, but it was

254

as if it had turned into an echo. In a way, they were inside the waterfall.

"Heidi?" Astrid called again, as she felt she'd walked quite some distance now without seeing anything. She couldn't believe it: there she was, in a secret passage! It was absolutely incredible.

And then there was suddenly light. Astrid almost fell over a kind of step going down. She'd entered a cave. A massive cave! There had to be space for thirty people inside. The little thunderbolt of Glimmerdal stood there gaping. She was speechless. A cave! A cave in Glimmerdal!

"Welcome to my secret," said Heidi, smiling and gesturing with her arms. She'd lit some candles so they could see each other. "Not even Sigurd knows about this place," she added with a wink.

And then, while Astrid stood there in the middle of the cave, still totally speechless, Heidi opened her orange backpack and took out the fiddle.

Astrid Glimmerdal will remember that moment for the rest of her life, as clear as water, every single second like a diamond in her mind. After Heidi had tuned Gunnvald's fiddle and tucked it under her chin, the most fantastic thing Astrid had ever experienced happened.

Heidi played to the river.

Behind them, above them, and around them, they could taste and smell the river, and as Heidi drew her bow across the strings, the notes mingled with the sound of the water. Goose bumps rippled across Astrid's body. She was surrounded by music.

When the notes finally died away, Astrid was still speechless. Heidi smiled.

"I used to play here when I was little. I found the cave purely by chance one summer when I stayed at Glimmerdal Shieling for almost a week and thought I should try having a shower in the waterfall."

"Wow" was all Astrid could say, quite faintly.

"And you know, Astrid, I've played music all over the world, but all I've longed for that whole time has been to come here and play in my river cave again."

Astrid could understand that.

"Try singing 'Bluey, Billy Goat of Mine,'" said Heidi.

Astrid didn't need to be asked twice. She sang to her heart's content while Heidi played. When they finished, Astrid had to sit down.

"That's the most beautiful thing I've ever heard," she said blissfully.

Heidi laughed.

They didn't speak on their way home: they were so full of secrets and music that words weren't enough. But when they reached Gunnvald's farm, Astrid cleared her throat ceremoniously.

"Heidi, would you like to come to my birthday party on Easter Sunday?"

Heidi turned around, surprised. "Really? How old are you going to be?"

"Ten. It's a round-number birthday," Astrid announced.

"That's quite something, Astrid Glimmerdal. Quite something indeed."

Heidi lifted the fiddle case out of her orange backpack. "Now you can take this to Gunnvald."

CHAPTER TWENTY-SEVEN

In which Snorri the Seagull gets a seagull castle, and Gunnvald comes home

I t's my birthday in just over a week; tomorrow Ola, Broder, and Birgitte are coming to Glimmerdal for their Easter vacation; and today . . ." Astrid stopped to catch her breath. "Today Gunnvald's coming home. And he'll be reunited with Heidi!"

Astrid was lying in bed and had so many things to look forward to that she could hardly get up.

As she lay there, so happy and excited that she almost felt ill, Astrid heard a noise that made her leap out of bed. It sounded like somebody revving and tuning moped engines. She rushed over to her attic window. At first, she was so surprised that she thought she was dreaming. Down in the farmyard were two skinny legs, in jeans full of holes, sticking out from beneath a moped. And not far away was the back of a green checkered shirt, leaning over another moped.

Astrid threw the window wide open. "Auntie Eira! Auntie Idun!"

Astrid thought that God must have been having a good day when he made her aunties.

"Today I'm going to come up with a surprise," said God, and then he started putting together an auntie.

He made her skinny and freckly, and decided that she would crumple up like an accordion when she laughed. Then he stuffed her full of noise. He'd never put so much noise in an aunt before, Astrid thought. God decided that she would like everything that was funny, everything that made loud bangs, and everything that moved fast. When he'd finished, he took a step back and looked at that aunt. He'd never seen anything like her. He was so pleased with her that he decided to make another, so by the end of the day, God had made two aunts who looked exactly the same. To put the icing on the cake, he took an extra fistful of freckles from his freckle bowl and sprinkled them all over both of them, especially on their knees.

"Knee freckles are my favorite thing," said God.

Astrid imagined he must have pondered for a while who he should give the aunts to, since they'd make such a racket. Eventually he put them in Astrid's granny's tummy. She already had four boys who were getting big by then, so she was quite experienced. Astrid's granny called the first aunt Idun and the second Eira. She thought they were the most beautiful things she'd ever seen. She'd told Astrid that. Then, from heaven, God looked after her aunts, just like he does all aunts. But Astrid thought he must have had to keep a special eye on these ones, since they got up to all sorts of mischief. He must have sat up there chuckling to himself, and when they were ten, God decided to give the aunts a surprise.

"And then, with a big fanfare, da-da-da-da-da-*daa,* along came the little thunderbolt of Glimmerdal, with freckles on her knees," Astrid always said when she told her aunts the story. It was all so well thought out by God that she really couldn't have made it up any better herself.

And now Astrid's aunts had come home several days earlier than planned. They'd heard rumors that the snow in Glimmerdal was melting at an outrageous speed that year, they said, so if they wanted to do any real skiing, they'd have to whizz home. On top of that, they'd also heard that big brother of theirs was getting worn out with the lambing.

"And last, but by no means least," said Auntie Idun, "we heard that Astrid Glimmerdal's got a big birthday coming up and is going to have a massive party, and things like that take some planning. What kind of cakes do we need to bake?"

Astrid smiled a smile as wide as a bus. "Well, I did promise Snorri I'd make him a seagull's castle out of real gingerbread," she said.

After breakfast, Astrid and her aunts carried the ingredients they'd need over to the old house. That quiet house was going to liven up now: Astrid's aunts always filled it with friends and all sorts of hullabaloo. Most of all, they filled it with Peter. Astrid knew he'd be coming soon. He'd park his Volvo over by the barn and walk calmly across the farmyard with his lopsided smile. And even though Gunnvald had told Peter to get his act together on the love front, he probably wasn't going to be able to spit it out this Easter either that he was in love with Auntie Idun, and that he'd been in love with her since their second year at elementary school. In other words, for twelve years.

"If I ever fall in love, although I doubt I will, I'll certainly make sure to tell the person in question," Astrid had told Gunnvald the last time they'd spoken about it.

"Mozart above," Gunnvald had said.

Over in the old house, Auntie Eira climbed up onto the kitchen counter and took down the world's largest mixing bowl. Then they got to work, spreading a billowing cloud of flour through the cold kitchen.

"I think there must be some kind of curse on gingerbread made so far out of season. You know, we normally make gingerbread at Christmas," said Auntie Idun as Astrid smashed her third egg outside the enormous mixing bowl.

It went *blop* as it landed on the counter. Snorri sat watching them from Astrid's grandpa's rocking chair. He gave a *"Squaaawk!"* every time the eggs went *blop*.

"Maybe he thinks I'm smashing seagull eggs," Astrid realized. She told Snorri to look away if he thought it was disgusting.

Astrid and Auntie Eira dreamed up all the things the castle would need. Auntie Idun drew designs and did the math to work out what was possible. Gingerbread pieces were put in and taken out of the oven tray by tray.

"With all this gingerbread, we're going to confuse Santa. What if he comes stumbling along here in April?" said Auntie Eira, taking a really deep breath of the gingerbread smell.

There were bits of gingerbread covering all the tables and countertops in the kitchen. Now they needed the sugar mixture to stick the pieces together.

"Take two steps backward, please," Auntie Eira commanded as she got going with the red-hot gooey mixture.

Astrid had never been part of making such a huge

263

gingerbread castle before. When they put the last piece
into place, it was almost a meter and a half tall, with three
floors, four balconies, two towers, and a rickety walkway.
They'd even made a flagpole. It looked like it might collapse
if you so much as glanced at it the wrong way, but Auntie
Eira swore that her sugar mixture was better than all the
superglue in the world.

"Snorri's going to live like a king in there!" she said.

And that was when Astrid suddenly glanced at
the clock. It was half past three. How could that have
happened?

"Gunnvald!" she shouted.

How could she have gotten so caught up that she'd
forgotten? And Heidi, what about her? Suddenly Astrid
was in such a hurry that she didn't know where to start.
Big things were about to happen. She hustled out into the
corridor, crashing into Peter, who was on his way in.

Astrid's dad had already started the car. He was going
to fetch Gunnvald from the ferry and wondered whether
Astrid wanted to come along for the ride. She shook her
head. She had to go and find Heidi! Her lion curls danced

in the spring sunlight. Imagine how strange it was going to be: Gunnvald and Heidi, father and daughter. They hadn't seen each other in almost thirty years! Astrid ran down the hill as fast as she could.

But as soon as she arrived at Gunnvald's farm, she sensed that something wasn't as it should be. Was it the dark windows, perhaps? Or the way the house was looking at her? Maybe the fact that it was so terribly quiet? Astrid rushed up the steps to the house and threw the door open.

"Heidi?"

Nobody answered.

She ran all through the house: up and down stairs, through Gunnvald's thousand sitting rooms, the bedrooms, the workshop, the garage, the barn. She shouted and shouted, but nobody answered. Neither the puppy nor Heidi was anywhere to be seen.

And then she found the note on the kitchen table. "Thank you for everything," it said.

Astrid was speechless. She stood by the kitchen table, reading the note over and over again.

Heidi was gone.

*   *   *

When Astrid's dad and Gunnvald drove into the farmyard, Astrid was sitting on the steps outside the house. Wet trails of tears lined her cheeks.

Astrid's dad helped Gunnvald out of the car. The enormous Gunnvald stood there, looking at his farm, his house, and his glen, all of which he'd missed so much, but most of all, he looked at Astrid with her tear-streaked face.

Then it was as if he snapped: it was so horrible to watch that it felt as if somebody were crushing Astrid's heart. With a small whimper, she stood up from the steps and ran across the farmyard. She threw her arms around her enormous best friend's stomach, more or less where he seemed most broken, and buried her face in his jacket. She hugged him so he would know how much she loved him.

They stood there like that, Astrid and Gunnvald, while spring sprang around them and the river filled the air with its loud, mournful lament.

CHAPTER TWENTY-EIGHT

In which Auntie Eira skis a somersault, Astrid almost skis a somersault, and Ola is nowhere near skiing a somersault

Are we going all the way up there?" Ola asked, pointing his ski pole toward the top of Cairn Peak.

Astrid shook her head. "Are you crazy? You've got to learn to ski first. Don't forget: you have to come back down too."

"I do know how to ski!" Ola shouted angrily.

"But you're not very good," Astrid replied, being honest.

"Yes, I am!"

Behind them, Broder laughed quietly.

Ola, Broder, Birgitte, and their mom had returned to

Glimmerdal. The spring thaw had moved them farther up the mountain than the last time they'd come, but Mr. Hagen could probably still hear them if he listened extra carefully. They could hardly have a quiet time up there in the Easter snow when it was only the fourth occasion in his life that Ola had put on skis.

Astrid went at the front, leaving a trail for them to follow in the wet snow. After a while, she met a ski trail that was already there. When she lifted her head, she could see who had made it.

"Now you'll see somebody who really knows how to ski," she told Ola, pointing up at the two black dots beneath the summit of Cairn Peak.

"Who's that?" asked Broder.

"My aunties," said Astrid proudly.

The side of Cairn Peak is Auntie Eira and Auntie Idun's favorite slope.

"There's something wrong with you," Astrid's grandpa always tells them. "Why can't you stay on the flat parts like everyone else?"

But if Astrid's aunts had stayed on the flat parts like

everyone else, the little thunderbolt of Glimmerdal wouldn't have been able to enjoy the music that played in her head as she watched them come dancing down the slope, like now. Besides, her grandpa wouldn't be coming home until later in the Easter vacation.

Auntie Idun was the best skier. The track behind her was as straight as an arrow, as if somebody had drawn a finger through the snow. Auntie Eira skied more in fits and starts, but she was the best one at jumping. And now she was approaching the Little Hammer at top speed.

Astrid watched with her mouth wide open as Auntie Eira's lean body pretty much flopped off the edge of the Little Hammer and leaned back. Calmly and smoothly, with her arms and ski poles sticking straight out like slender wings, Auntie Eira stretched into an endless somersault before landing softly below the Little Hammer. Auntie Idun followed her. She didn't do a somersault; she just pulled in her legs and flew far, far through the air like a little ball. It looked as easy as anything.

"Wow," Ola whispered.

"Yup," said Astrid. Then she started singing "Old

MacDonald" as she heaved herself along.

It was no good this time either. Astrid landed on her back beneath the Little Hammer with a real slam, winding herself. If she didn't die now, she never would!

"You've gotten really good!" said Auntie Idun, smiling and calmly rubbing Astrid's chest until she could get her breath back.

Astrid was about to reply but was interrupted by a howl of the worst kind imaginable. It was Ola. He came flapping through the sky like a crow: skis, ski poles, hands, and feet pointing in all directions.

"Somebody's got the hang of it," Auntie Eira murmured, her eyes following the little Easter visitor's trajectory through the air.

Broder came snowplowing down to them, just in time to see his little brother crash-land in the damp spring snow.

"OOOOOWWW!"

A little later, Astrid stood at the door and watched as Gunnvald cleaned the graze on Ola's cheek. Birgitte was playing with Hulda in the slants of sunlight on the kitchen floor. The boys' mother was baking buns. It all looked like a beautiful, shiny photograph: it was Easter, there were guests, and there was plenty of joyful noise. But beneath all this happiness was something not so happy. Where was Heidi? Astrid could see in Gunnvald's eyes that he was thinking about it the whole time. She was thinking about it the whole time too. Heidi, Heidi, Heidi.

They'd tried to find her, but the only thing they knew was that she'd left on the boat and was going to catch a flight: Able Seaman Jon had told them that much. That flight could have been going anywhere. They hadn't managed to find any phone numbers that worked either. Nobody answered when they called the number they'd found for the house in Frankfurt, and a cell phone number they tracked down was no longer in service. Astrid's mom was able to get in touch with Heidi's agent: he was the one who organized all of her concerts. But the agent told her that Heidi had taken an indeterminate leave of absence. He hadn't heard from her for a long time. It was as if Heidi had vanished off the face of the earth.

"She doesn't want to be found," Astrid's dad said in the end. He told them they should stop looking.

But how could they stop looking? Astrid couldn't understand. Seeing Gunnvald like that broke her heart. The worst thing of all, the thing that made Astrid more worried than anything on earth, was that Gunnvald no longer played his fiddle. He hadn't touched it since he'd come home: it just hung there on the wall, silent and dead. That had never happened before. No matter how bad things were, Gunnvald had always played his fiddle. His fiddle used to make him feel better when nothing else worked.

Astrid couldn't imagine what would have happened if the little family hadn't come for their Easter break. Thanks to them, the days went by, as days do.

She still had her birthday coming up soon, Astrid thought occasionally, almost dreading it now. Then she would have to smile in spite of all the gloom. She was even going to celebrate it over two days in a row: first on Saturday, when her real birthday was, and then on Sunday, when they were going to have their big combined spring–Easter–birthday party.

* * *

By the evening of Good Friday, there was only one more night left of being nine. Astrid lay in her bed and felt her warm cheeks throbbing. She must have gotten a little sunburned. But that wasn't what was keeping her awake. It was all her thoughts. The next day, she was going to be turning ten. She was going to be woken with cake and presents. She knew that. But she just lay there, tossing and turning. Eventually she got up and looked out her window.

She knew it. She'd felt it. The lamp was lit over in the summerhouse, though the night air was still and hushed.

Gunnvald sat with his back to the door. The summerhouse looked too small for him. Astrid sat down on the cold wooden bench, right next to him.

"Goodness. For heaven's sake, is that you, Astrid? Up and about in the middle of the night?"

"Yes."

They didn't say anything for a long while.

"It's your birthday tomorrow, you know," Gunnvald grumbled eventually.

"Yes. Do you know what I'm wishing for?"

"It's no good coming over here and wishing for something at one o'clock in the morning!" Gunnvald said irritably. "You must realize I've already bought you a present."

"Yes, but do you know what I'm wishing for?"

"Listen, I don't care what you're wishing for, because I've already bought you a present."

"Yes, but Gunnvald, don't you want to know what I'm wishing for more than anything?" Astrid asked him defiantly.

"No."

"I'm going to tell you anyway."

Gunnvald had no doubt she would. Astrid gave him a long look, her eyes pleading with him. Then she said, "I wish you'd play the fiddle again."

A ewe bleated inside the barn. The river kept on roaring.

"Bah, what a pain all that music is," Gunnvald moaned. "Liv called from the church today. She was wondering if I'd play at the service on Easter Sunday. She can dream on!"

"She asked you that?" Astrid sat up straight.

274

"The organist has broken his thigh bone," said Gunnvald. "As if he were the only one," he added, seeming offended.

"Come on, of course you want to play in church on Easter Sunday!" Astrid said eagerly. "The choir from Barkvika will probably be there too!"

"I don't give a lemming's tail about the choir from Barkvika."

"Yes, you do."

Astrid pictured Gunnvald when he played with the big choir from Barkvika. The last time, at Christmas, Astrid had sat in the gallery and watched as Gunnvald became one with the music. His tall rickety body had come so alive with the music that it was a joy to behold. When the choir sang the last verse of "Fair Is Creation," the swell of their voices and the notes from the fiddle were so strong that the church almost couldn't contain them.

"You're my godfather, Gunnvald. You're supposed to take me to church every now and then," Astrid lectured him. "And you should play your fiddle," she added. "It's wrong not to play it."

Then Gunnvald turned and looked at her, his eyes full of sadness. "I can't play anymore, Astrid. I don't have the music in me."

The words came pouring out of Gunnvald. He felt like the worst person in the world, he said, holding his big uncombed head in his hands. He'd acted like a troll toward Heidi, even though he was her father. And now it was too late to do anything about it. She'd left.

"Do you know how much I want to tell her I'm sorry, Astrid? I want to say sorry for having been such a fool. Sorry for letting her go. Sorry for everything. You know?"

Gunnvald's voice was so gloomy that it made Astrid gulp. She stared out into the darkness for a while, and then she turned toward him.

"Gunnvald, you're not the worst person in the world. I think you're the best," she said truthfully. "You're my best friend."

Gunnvald cleared his throat a little.

"And you're my godfather," she added, looking at him sternly. "So I suppose you should really take me to church occasionally."

"Rotten child," Gunnvald grumbled.

He got up and vanished into the darkness. Astrid heard him walk across the farmyard. She caught a quick glimpse of him under the outside light by the steps, and then he disappeared into the slumbering house. When he came back, he had his fiddle with him.

"I suppose I can say it, since it's after midnight," he grumbled. "Happy birthday, Astrid Glimmerdal."

He fell silent for a while, as if he were waiting for the music to come floating down from the night sky. But then, finally, he lifted the bow to the strings and began playing. For the first time since he'd come home, there was music in Glimmerdal.

And while the tender notes of "Bluey, Billy Goat of Mine" drifted out across the glen, Astrid sat there, knowing that everything would be fine, no matter what. Before she sleepily shuffled back home in the dark, she got Gunnvald to promise he would play in church too. She knew that he really wanted to, deep down. Honestly, what would he do without her?

CHAPTER TWENTY-NINE

In which Astrid turns ten, receives a big crate, and has a brain wave

I t's just as well everybody has a birthday, including Astrid. She was sitting up in bed, smiling from ear to ear. On top of her quilt was a tray with cream cake for breakfast, and there were presents all around her from all of the family.

"I'm the happiest person in the world," she sighed.

When breakfast was done with, she went out for a stroll in the farmyard. She'd invited Ola and Broder to come and spend the whole day with her. But when she looked down the hill, she saw something quite different from two brothers. She saw a big truck coming out of the enchanted forest by Sally's house. At the bridge, the truck turned up onto the track to Astrid's farm. What on earth had her dad ordered now? The monster of a truck stopped in the middle of the farmyard, rumbling with its engine running idle. A man jumped out.

"Astrid Glimmerdal?" he said.

She nodded.

"Can you sign here, please?"

He held a piece of paper out in front of her. Astrid didn't know how to sign for something. The man explained that she had to write her name on the piece of paper so she could receive the crate he had for her in the truck. That's what signing for something means.

"I haven't ordered any crate," said Astrid.

"Maybe not, but I've been asked to deliver it to you," the man explained impatiently, holding a pen right up to her nose.

Astrid wasn't going to protest, so she took the pen and signed "Astrid Glimmerdal," and when the truck had driven off down the hill, there was a massive crate left in the middle of the farmyard.

279

Ola and Broder came into view as the dust settled.

"What have you got there?" asked Ola.

Astrid scratched her head. She had no idea. But one thing was certain: she'd never received anything this big before. The three children approached the crate curiously, but then they all jumped at the same time. There was something moving inside! What on earth could it be?

"Take off the lid!" Ola was beside himself with excitement.

Working together, they managed to lift it off.

"Animals!" Ola shouted.

Inside the crate were a goat and two little goat kids.

"Oh!" exclaimed Astrid. "But who . . . ?"

She turned around, as now her whole family had come out into the farmyard to see what was going on. They all looked equally surprised. None of them had ordered any goats.

Astrid's dad and mom lifted the kids carefully out of the crate.

"These are two billy goats," said Astrid's dad, stroking one of them gently.

Taking care, they put the goat kids down on the ground. The mother goat looked up skeptically at all the faces peering into the crate.

"There's a note," said Broder, passing it to Astrid.

Dear Astrid,
I'm sending you Bluey and the teeny-tiniest billy goat Gruff, and their mother, old Lucky. I know they'll like it in Glimmerdal. Have a happy tenth birthday.
Best wishes,
Heidi

Astrid read the note several times. Heidi. Just think: she'd remembered her birthday, sent her two live billy goats and a mother goat, and even remembered what their names should be: Bluey, the teeny-tiniest billy goat Gruff, and old Lucky. Astrid had told Heidi the story and sung her the song, and now she was stunned speechless. She felt something so big and warm inside her that she didn't know what to do. Slowly she knelt and reached out her hands.

"Come on," she said softly, calling the billy goats to her.

They were afraid, but Bluey came first, and then the teeny-tiniest billy goat Gruff followed. They sniffed her hands, and Astrid felt it tickle as they touched her fingers.

"Heidi," she whispered.

Astrid wanted to tell Gunnvald about this herself.

"You can help Auntie Eira and Auntie Idun decorate the seagull's castle," she suggested to Ola and Broder.

Then she set off strolling down the hill. Bluey and the teeny-tiniest billy goat Gruff had already figured out who owned them, and they came toddling along behind her. Astrid was quite touched. Old Lucky sauntered at the back. She sniffed around all over the side of the track and still seemed quite skeptical after their long journey in the truck.

"We're going up to see Gunnvald. He's the father of the woman who sent you here," Astrid explained.

She had to stop down at the bridge to hear what it sounded like when the billy goats went across. She got them to go back and forth several times. It was more *click-plack* than *trip-trap,* Astrid thought. She could hardly believe it: they were her goats! She'd never wanted to thank somebody as much as she did now. For the first time, she really understood what Gunnvald must feel like, having so much to say to Heidi but no way of telling her. Oh, if only they could call her!

That's when it suddenly hit Astrid like lightning: Mr. Hagen!

Mr. Hagen *had* to have a phone number for Heidi. Astrid herself had heard him call her.

"Come on!" she shouted to her new animals.

In the flower bed outside Mr. Hagen's reception, there were neat rows of blue and orange crocuses. Astrid had to stop and admire them for a moment. If only Sally could see them! Prickly puffins, that man really knew what he was doing when it came to flowers.

Mr. Hagen was sitting behind his desk. Astrid told her animals to wait outside, but Bluey sneaked into reception before she could shut the door.

"You've got to wait outside," Astrid explained.

It was a real struggle getting Bluey to understand, though, and when she finally shooed him out, he'd left a couple of small round droppings on the doormat. Imagine pooping in Mr. Hagen's reception. What a goat!

"Yes?" asked Mr. Hagen when Astrid had finished dealing with the goats and kicked the droppings onto the steps outside.

She went right up to the desk and rested her chin on it. "It's my birthday today."

Mr. Hagen couldn't have looked less interested.

"Don't you think it's a good thing that I'm starting to get on a bit in years?" Astrid asked him sincerely. Surely it had to be good news for Mr. Hagen that she had a little less of her childhood left.

"What do you want?"

It clearly wasn't a day for small talk.

"I was wondering whether you had Heidi's phone number."

"So that's what you want?" Mr. Hagen said scornfully. "You're going to call her and thank her for spoiling all my plans, are you?"

"No, I'm going to thank her for something else," Astrid explained.

But Mr. Hagen wasn't listening. "I bet you're happy,

young Asny, now that you've stopped that farm sale, aren't you? Eh? Happy, are you?"

Astrid lifted her chin off the desk so she could nod. There was no point in lying.

"Do you know how fed up I am with this blasted Glimmerdal of yours?" Mr. Hagen asked her.

Astrid shook her head.

"I'm so blinking fed up that I could puke," he shouted. "This whole place is populated by reactionary yokels! It's impossible to get anything done."

Astrid stood there, wishing that she could understand Mr. Hagen. Yokels? Did he mean her, Gunnvald, her dad, Sally, Nils, and people like them?

"Hey, Klaus," she said softly. "I'd be really grateful if I could have that phone number."

She got it. He scrolled through the numbers on his phone and scrawled one of them on a piece of paper.

"I talked to her yesterday, actually," he muttered. "That obstinate woman," he added, pushing the piece of paper over to Astrid.

Mr. Hagen had no idea what an angel he was, giving

Astrid that number. As a result, he was extremely surprised by what happened next. Astrid walked all the way around the desk and gave him a real bear-crusher of a hug. Nothing like that had ever happened to Mr. Hagen before. He was completely tongue-tied.

"Thank you so much! This is the best birthday present I've had," Astrid said truthfully. It was no small matter saying something like that when she'd already been given two live billy goats and a whole grown-up mother goat too.

"See ya!"

Astrid didn't notice that her new pets had made a real mess out of the crocuses in the flower bed while she'd been inside. There was no time to worry about things like that. Mr. Hagen didn't notice it either, not until Astrid and her goats were deep into the enchanted forest. He sat in his chair instead, scratching his head.

"There's something wrong with the people in this place," he grumbled.

CHAPTER THIRTY

In which Gunnvald makes the most important telephone call of his life

C an you keep an eye on the animals, please?" Astrid asked, panting at Birgitte and her mother when she reached Gunnvald's farm. Then she staggered into the kitchen. "Gu . . . hunnvald . . ." she gasped. She held out the scrap of paper.

"Come here; I've got something for you," said Gunnvald.

Astrid didn't care about that. She waved the piece of paper in front of him. "Gunnvald, I—"

Gunnvald didn't see the paper. "Look at this," he said, pulling out a box from the corner behind the door.

Astrid still couldn't think of anything other than the

note she held in her hand. "Gunnvald, I've got something important—"

But Gunnvald became angry. "What could be more important than this? Open your birthday present, Astrid!"

It was another big box. If she hadn't already been given two billy goats and a nanny goat, this box would've seemed massive. Astrid put the scrap of paper in her pocket. It could wait another five minutes. With trembling fingers, she started to tear off the paper. There was a wooden box inside. Gunnvald was sitting on the edge of a kitchen chair, watching excitedly.

When Astrid opened the wooden box and saw what was inside, she fell silent.

"You know, I wanted to give you the best thing I could," he said.

Astrid was still quiet. She stroked a finger across the shiny green object in the box. An accordion. Gunnvald had given her a real accordion to play music with. It was such a tremendous thing that she was afraid of what might come out if she opened her mouth.

"Don't you like it?" he asked.

"Gunnvald," Astrid whispered, "I love it." She stumbled across the floor and threw her arms around his neck. "Now I can play music too! We can play together, Gunnvald!"

Gunnvald smiled heartily when he saw how happy she was. It was the first time Astrid had seen him smile properly since he'd fallen down the steps outside his house what felt like a thousand years ago. She stood there for a while, sunbathing in his smile, and then she fished the scrap of paper out of her pocket with great solemnity.

"Gunnvald, I've got Heidi's phone number," she said.

It isn't easy to make a phone call when you've waited almost thirty years to do it. Astrid could understand that. Of course it was a big, scary, and difficult thing, but Gunnvald *had* to do it.

He walked back and forth in the kitchen like an elk in a cage, his hand moving through his hair, across his chest, and then suddenly out into the air. He couldn't do it. It was impossible. He felt as if he were about to have a heart attack.

"It won't get any better if you wait another thirty years," Astrid told him sternly. "You've *got* to do it!"

But Gunnvald was beside himself with worry. "Heidi doesn't want to be found. You heard Sigurd himself say it!" he shouted.

Then Astrid stamped her foot, sending the picture of Gunnvald's grandfather and the beautiful Madelene Katrine Benedicte falling onto the sofa.

"Heidi's been waiting all her life for you to call her. Blinking badgers, you're her father!"

Gunnvald gave in and picked up the telephone.

Astrid would never have thought someone could tremble so much. She sat close to him, holding his free hand as he dialed the number on his big old telephone. It rang once. Neither Astrid nor Gunnvald was breathing. It rang a second time. Astrid gulped, and Gunnvald slowly shifted his weight. It rang a third time, and then they heard a crackle at the other end.

"Hello, this is Heidi."

Gunnvald's body froze stiff like a fork.

"Hello? Who is it?" asked Heidi.

Astrid prodded Gunnvald and looked at him urgently. He opened his mouth wide, but not a sound came out.

"Gunnvald!" Astrid whispered desperately, shaking him.

He opened and closed his mouth three more times. And then he hung up, slamming down the receiver.

Astrid couldn't believe it. She stared at the telephone and then at Gunnvald. "You oaf!" she blurted out. "Why didn't you say anything?"

Gunnvald put his elbows on the table and buried his head in his enormous hands. "I don't know what to say, Astrid. I have no idea how to say what I need to say."

Behind his hands, he was totally crushed. Astrid slumped and looked out the window. What now? Why did everything have to be so difficult?

She turned around and stared at Gunnvald again. Then she climbed up onto her chair to reach the fiddle and put it on the table in front of them. "Go on, play."

Astrid dialed the number on the scrap of paper one more time, and when she heard a slightly impatient Heidi answer, she nodded to Gunnvald. Then she lifted up her arm and held out the receiver at the same time as the old troll of Glimmerdal lifted his fiddle and brought the bow up to the strings.

*　　*　　*

Astrid had heard Gunnvald play many times. His music had been in the air around her all her life, for as long as she could remember, but she'd never heard Gunnvald play like he was doing now. He stood there in the kitchen, as usual. His hair was tousled, as usual. His eyes were closed, as usual. But what came out of his fiddle wasn't the same as usual. It was as if Gunnvald were putting his whole heart into the music. He was playing for Heidi. And he played for a long time. Gunnvald played out all he had inside him.

When he finished, it was quieter than Astrid could ever remember anything being before. Shaking, she lifted the receiver up to her ear.

Click.

Heidi had hung up.

CHAPTER THIRTY-ONE

In which everybody, except for Ola, goes to church

No, I don't want to!"

Ola was in the corner of the kitchen. He'd put on a shirt and tie, but he wasn't going any further. He didn't want to go to church under any circumstances.

"The choir's going to sing, and Gunnvald's going to play his fiddle. It'll be fun," Astrid insisted.

"I've been to church before!" said Ola. "It's not fun. It's boring."

Astrid sighed. Ola grabbed the large bread knife that was on the kitchen counter and waved it in the air. "I'll guard the house."

"As you wish," she said.

*   *   *

It was beautiful outside the church in Barkvika. The sun made the yellow daffodils shine. Astrid noticed that people were happy when they saw Gunnvald had his fiddle case with him. But Gunnvald wasn't smiling. He just stood there glaring in the sunlight with his fiddle case in his hand, his shoulders hunched as if he were broken. He'd hardly said a word since the phone had gone *click* the day before.

When everybody was inside, Astrid took him by the hand. "Gunnvald?"

"Mmm?"

"At least you've called her now."

They both stopped there. Gunnvald crouched down, his thigh creaking, and he placed his two gigantic hands on Astrid's shoulders.

"What would I do without you, Astrid Glimmerdal?"

Astrid tried to shrug, but it wasn't exactly easy with such enormous hands resting on her shoulders. "You'd probably drop down dead," she said.

Gunnvald laughed. "I probably would," he roared.

"I probably would."

Then Astrid and Gunnvald went inside.

Astrid liked going to church when she could just sit in peace up there in the gallery, as she was doing now, looking at all the strange and beautiful things. She sat with her chin on the railing, gazing out across all the heads down below. She could see Broder and Birgitte, and their mother, together with her own mom and dad, and her aunts. Her granny and grandpa were also there. Later that evening would be the big party. Astrid was looking forward to it.

Gunnvald had already played several times during the service. Astrid thought his suit trousers were maybe looking even shorter than usual, but at least he'd sort of combed his hair.

Then came the last hymn that everybody would sing: "Easter Morrow Stills Our Sorrow." While Astrid was singing in a resounding voice, she suddenly became aware of somebody standing behind her. She could sense it. She turned around in surprise, and there, in the shadows by the stairs, was a person. A tall person.

"Heidi," Astrid whispered, her mouth wide open.

Heidi went up to where Astrid was sitting. She stood there as if she had turned to stone, staring down at the nave of the church. She watched Gunnvald play "Easter Morrow Stills Our Sorrow." She watched Gunnvald let the last quivering note wind its way through the chandeliers. She watched Gunnvald as he lowered his instrument and then stood there with his fiddle hanging in one hand and his bow in the other while Liv, the minister, thanked everybody for coming and blessed the congregation. Heidi watched Gunnvald as the church bells rang three sets of three peals. The congregation sat down, and Liv nodded to Gunnvald and the choir from Barkvika, giving them the signal to start playing the postlude, the final tune. But then Heidi stopped watching Gunnvald. She went back into the shadows by the stairs.

Astrid thought that Heidi was about to go. She couldn't! Astrid was just about to shout out to her when she saw that Heidi wasn't leaving. Instead Heidi bent down in the shadows and picked something up.

*   *   *

Gunnvald and the choir from Barkvika had gotten about halfway through the postlude when it happened. To begin with, nobody reacted, not even Gunnvald. But gradually people started to look around in astonishment. Fiddle music was coming from somewhere, matching Gunnvald's playing note for note, and doubling the volume.

Astrid watched as Gunnvald, without pausing, opened his eyes in amazement and lifted his head. Then his bow stopped moving. For a moment, Astrid was afraid his heart might stop too. He stood frozen. But then he closed his eyes tightly and started playing again, somehow. The music from the two instruments wove together around the choir's singing, filling the church right up to the roof and out into the spring air. When they finished, it was so quiet that Astrid was scared to breathe. Nobody had heard music like that before. The whole choir stared up at the tall woman in the gallery. But she was still only looking at Gunnvald.

And then, like clouds parting in the sky, Heidi's stern face opened, letting out a short glimpse of a smile. Gunnvald, that stubborn old mule, just stood there, peering up at that smile from under his toothbrush-like eyebrows.

That was when Astrid Glimmerdal started clapping. She clapped like a madwoman. She couldn't remember the last time she'd been so happy!

Astrid led Heidi through the crowd of people outside the church. Gunnvald had hardly dared to step outside. He stood at the church door, emotion written all over his face.

"Here she is," announced Astrid.

Heidi smiled again, briefly. It seemed that neither she nor Gunnvald really knew what to say, but they didn't have to spend too long thinking about it, because they all suddenly heard a colossal racket. A door slammed in the parking lot, someone shouted, "Thanks for the ride!" so loudly that it echoed, and then the wrought-iron gate to the churchyard opened with a crash.

It was Ola. He ran between all the people. "Astrid!" His shirt was hanging out, and his tie was dangling behind him like a tail. "She's come back! The monster woman's come back!"

Ola grabbed Astrid's arm. "That monster woman with the dog is—"

He stopped dead. The monster woman was standing right next to them. For a brief moment, he was completely silent, then he took in a breath and pointed furiously at Heidi.

"You sold the farm! I saw it with my own eyes!"

It was strangely quiet among the people outside the church: all eyes were on the little group with Ola and Heidi in the middle. Ola's chest was rising and falling like a small set of bellows.

"She came up to the farm and asked for Gunnvald. I told her you were at church and I was guarding the house. And I was too! I ran after her."

Ola told Astrid that he'd been spying to try and find out where Heidi had gone, and when he got down to the vacation camp, he saw that her car was there.

"I was lying in the flower bed and I heard it all. The window was open. She's sold the farm! I was supposed to be on the lookout, but . . ."

Ola was so angry that he was crying. He managed to

299

gasp in between his tears that he promised he'd run as fast as he could.

"But it was too late. That man at the camp said thank you for doing business with him, and she said she hoped he was pleased."

Then Ola couldn't say any more. He roared instead and launched himself at the monster woman. Heidi stopped him as easily as she'd stopped Astrid that time she'd attacked her.

"Are you denying it?" Ola shouted furiously, as Heidi held him in her tight grip. "You wrote your name on a piece of paper and thanked him! Are you denying it?" he screamed.

Heidi put him down. "No, I'm not denying it, I . . ."

Gunnvald's face had gone gray, and Astrid could feel all her strength leaving her.

"Heidi," she whispered, "Mr. Hagen is going to ruin everything. You promised not to do it." Astrid couldn't say any more.

Heidi swallowed. "Mr. Hagen isn't going to ruin—" she started.

"Yes, he is! You know it!" Astrid shouted, no longer trying to hold back the tears. She started sobbing uncontrollably, right outside the church.

"Stop crying; it's not like that," said Heidi, embarrassed as she looked at all the people around them. She wiped away a couple of Astrid's tears decisively.

"Stop crying, I said. I've bought the vacation camp, Astrid."

CHAPTER THIRTY-TWO

In which two fiddles
play together

"Now things are going to get lively!" Auntie Eira shouted as the first car drove up into the farmyard.

And things really did get lively. Soon the whole house was full of people. Ola and Broder got to meet Andrea and the others from Astrid's class, who had come all the way from Barkvika. Peter had brought old Nils and Granny Anna, and Astrid's mom and dad had invited their friends. Sally came in her Sunday best. She'd bought Astrid an exquisite glass angel. It was a long time since so many people had been gathered up there.

The best thing of all was that Heidi was there. Astrid felt happy in her stomach every time she saw her. Heidi didn't say very much, and neither did Gunnvald. But they had their fiddles. Later in the evening, Astrid's dad cleared the living-room floor of furniture, and then Heidi and Gunnvald played dance music. Astrid took out her accordion and played with them.

"You sound like an asthmatic elephant!" Auntie Eira shouted, putting her hands over her ears.

"But I'm sure you'll get better in time," Auntie Idun reassured her.

When it was almost one o'clock and the first guests had gone home, Astrid, Broder, and Ola settled down on the sofa where Heidi was sitting.

"Have you really, really bought the camp?" Astrid asked.

Heidi nodded. It seemed Mr. Hagen was fed up with Glimmerdal, she said.

Ola looked in another direction.

"What?" he shouted angrily when he noticed that they were laughing. "How was I supposed to know? It's hardly a normal thing to go and buy a wellness retreat, is it? What are you going to do with it, anyway?" he asked irritably.

"I thought I could run it, at least for some of the year," said Heidi. "And then I'm sure I can find somebody to look after it when I'm traveling."

"Will children be allowed there?" Broder wondered.

"Yes."

"Noisy ones too?" asked Ola.

"Especially noisy ones," Heidi promised.

Ola smiled and leaped off the sofa. "And tonight we're going to sleep outside, aren't we, Astrid?"

They were. You bet they were!

When the party quieted down, Ola and Broder ran over to Gunnvald and Heidi's farm to fetch their woolly clothes, and Astrid had Heidi to herself for a little while.

"Are you going to spend any time with Gunnvald while you're in Glimmerdal?" she asked. She couldn't hide the worried tone in her voice.

Heidi glanced over at her gigantic father. He was chatting with Astrid's mom and dad. "Yes, I think I will," she said. "But I'll see how I feel."

Astrid nodded.

"You know, I've felt extremely angry at Gunnvald for

almost thirty years," said Heidi. "That's not something you can switch off just like that."

Astrid looked at Gunnvald and felt how terribly fond she was of him. Suddenly he turned toward the sofa where they were sitting. He put his hands in his suit trouser pockets and smiled.

"Gunnvald's happy now," Astrid told Heidi.

"You're right," said Heidi.

When the last guests were gone, Astrid took her sleeping bag with her out into the night. Ola and Broder had borrowed one each from Astrid's aunts. Tired and joking, they traipsed over to the edge of the forest, where they rolled out their ground mats on the soft moss. It was late, almost three o'clock.

"I'm going to stay up all night," said Ola. He'd barely zipped up his sleeping bag before they heard him snoring.

"What a guy," Broder mumbled, curling up. He gave Astrid one of his angelic smiles and was out like a light.

Astrid, ten years old, lay awake. The wind whispered and the river was singing in Glimmerdal, but after a while, she heard something else. She sat up slowly and looked over to the other side of the glen.

The summerhouse was lit up, and in the light there were two large silhouettes. Astrid snuggled back down into her sleeping bag, contented.

"What would they do without me?" she mumbled, closing her eyes.

And then the little thunderbolt of Glimmerdal fell asleep. The distant notes from two fiddles mingled with the soothing sounds of the river, making miracle music in the spring night.

Ski down from Glimmerdal to Mathildewick Cove for more small-town Norwegian adventures!

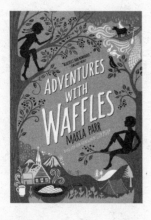

Nothing eases the pain of injury or the sting of parental disapproval like a batch of Auntie Granny's waffles, but when Lena keeps a huge secret from her best friend, Trille, there may not be enough waffles in the world to fix their friendship.

Available in hardcover, paperback, and audio and as an e-book

What are Trille and Lena to do when every raft they build sinks and every message in a bottle they send washes up on the shore at home? One thing is for sure: they're not giving up—not if Lena has anything to do with it!

Coming soon in hardcover, in audio, and as an e-book

The L-shaped breakwater in Mathildewick Cove is made of massive rocks and has a swimming area in the crook of its arm. In the winter, the storms blow in fine sand, which we use to make sandcastles and other fortifications. But when Lena went on vacation that summer, I'd been allowed to go with Minda and Magnus and their friends to the outside of the breakwater, where it's highest and the water below is deep and cold. It was almost like the beginning of a new life.

Lena's the champion of Mathildewick Cove when it comes to jumping off tall things. Nobody has less fear in

An excerpt from *Lena, the Sea, and Me*

their stomach. Or less sense in their head, as Magnus says. But even Lena's never jumped from the breakwater. She doesn't float very well.

"Throwing Lena into the fjord is more or less like dropping an anchor," says Grandpa.

It was quite a big deal that there was something I could jump from that she couldn't. I could tell that Lena wasn't pleased.

There I was on the highest rock on the breakwater. It was the crack of dawn, and it was only sixty degrees outside.

"Are you sure you're psyched up enough for this?" Lena asked me seriously.

She was leaning over one of the other rocks, wearing her jacket and a Mediterranean scarf. I nodded. I'd jumped in the water lots of times while she'd been away. But it had always been at high tide. Now the tide was out, and it was farther to jump. I could see the bottom. The wind buffeted my swimming shorts. For a moment I wondered whether it was really worth it. But then I saw Lena, back from Crete, leaning over the rock and not believing I could do it.

An excerpt from *Lena, the Sea, and Me*

I closed my eyes and took a deep breath. One. Two. THREE!

Ker-splash! came the sound as I hit the water, and then *sworlsh* as the bubbling surface closed over my head. The first time I'd gone down into the deep like this, I'd thought I was going to drown. Now I knew that all I had to do was thrash my legs around like crazy and hold my breath.

"Phuh!" I puffed as I shot back through the surface of the water and into the summer morning air.

Lena had climbed up onto the highest rock and was looking down at me skeptically. I smiled triumphantly. I'd shown her this time!

Next thing I knew, Lena was putting one foot in front of the other and slapping her hands against her face to psych herself up.

"Ay-ay-aaaaaaaaaah!" she howled.

Then she flew through the air in her jeans, sweater, jacket, scarf, and sneakers.

Ker-splash!

An excerpt from *Lena, the Sea, and Me*